'Tell me a... yours.'

'His name is To... voice.

'Tell me more.'

'He has fair hair and blue eyes. I have a picture, if you'd like to see it...'

Sterling was silent as she handed him the photo.

'He looks like you,' he said at last.

'Yes.'

His expression was stony. 'How old is Toby?'

'Three and a bit.'

Sterling took a quick step backwards. *'Three and a bit?'* he repeated disbelievingly. 'When was he born?'

'Sterling...'

'Nine months after we were together, Danielle?'

Kids...one of life's joys, one of life's treasures.

Kisses...of warmth, kisses of passion, kisses from mothers and kisses from lovers.

In *Kids and Kisses*...every story has it all.

Rosemary Carter was born in South Africa, but has lived in Canada for many years with her husband and her three children. Although her home is on the prairies, not far from the beautiful Rockies, she still retains her love of the South African bushveld, which is why she likes to set her stories there. Both Rosemary and her husband enjoy concerts, theatre, opera and hiking in the mountains. Reading was always her passion, and led to her first attempts at writing stories herself.

Recent titles by the same author:

TENDER CAPTIVE

FAMILY
MAN

BY
ROSEMARY CARTER

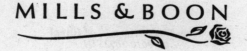

MILLS & BOON

MILLS & BOON and the Rose Device
are trademarks of the publisher.
Harlequin Mills & Boon Limited,
Eton House, 18-24 Paradise Road, Richmond, Surrey TW9 1SR

© Rosemary Carter 1996

ISBN 0 263 79798 8

Set in Times Roman 10 on 10½ pt.
02 -9610-58925 C1

Made and printed in Great Britain

CHAPTER ONE

DANIELLE saw him the moment she entered the chief executive's office. The man who was the new head of the company was standing by the windows at the far end of the spacious room, looking over the vista of downtown San Francisco.

A tall man, she noted, with broad shoulders and narrow hips, and glossy dark hair just touching the top of a white collar. There was something about the way he held himself, the slant of his neck, the tilt of his shoulders. Briefly memory stirred inside Danielle, then was still.

'Mr Tenassik.' Hugh Anderson, the office manager, cleared his throat. 'Miss Payne is here. If you'd like to dictate those memos now...'

The tall man turned from the window. He was smiling as he walked towards the desk. 'So much industry out there, we should be handling as much of the advertising as we possibly can,' he said to Hugh. 'We'll have to—'

The words stopped as his eyes lit on Danielle. Abruptly, he paused in mid-step, and just for a moment she thought the tanned face paled and the dark eyes revealed shock. Yet later, when she was able to think rationally once more, she wondered if it had only been her own shock she had felt.

Sterling! The name exploded in her throat, but did not make it past suddenly dry lips.

She was rooted to the floor as they stared at each other for a long moment. A timeless moment. And then, joy bursting forth inside her with all the force of fireworks lighting up a dark night sky, Danielle took a step forward.

In her dreams she had let herself imagine something like this happening; in the light of day she had known it never would. And yet here he was—Sterling, her beloved Sterling, and even more dynamic than she remembered him. Hugh Anderson forgotten, she was about to throw herself into Sterling's arms.

At that exact moment, Sterling said very politely, '*Miss Payne*, did you say, Hugh?'

The coldness of his tone hit her hard, striking her like a punch to the side of the head. The blood drained from her cheeks, and she put out a quick hand to the edge of the desk as she swayed on her feet.

'Miss Payne.' Sterling's right hand was outstretched.

Danielle stared at him, stunned. She had no idea why he was behaving so oddly. She was on the point of challenging him about it when she noticed the office manager, his eyes vivid with curiosity, watching them both. The question would have to wait.

'Danielle Payne,' she heard Hugh say. 'Danielle, this is our new chief executive, Sterling Tenassik.'

Strange now to remember that they had never known each other's surname. There had been a reason for it, of course. At their first meeting, fresh from the pain of a previous boyfriend's rejection and loth to suffer more of the same, Danielle had made it a condition that they revealed first names only. Later, when friendship had turned to passion, Sterling's attitude had made it difficult to reverse her terms.

His hand was still outstretched. Playing the game the way he seemed to want it played, Danielle made herself take it. His hand was warm, and as his fingers closed over hers a familiar tingling shot up her arm. For a moment a remembered hunger made her feel weak.

'Danielle is one of our best secretaries,' Hugh was saying.

'I'll be sure to bear that in mind.' There was politeness edged with mockery in Sterling's tone now as he addressed her. 'I take it you were Charlie Miller's private secretary, Miss Payne?'

'No,' she managed to say quite calmly, understanding that her manner had to be as detached as his own. 'We've always worked in a pool.'

'Interesting. And how long have you been with the company?'

'Almost four years.'

Something seemed to move in Sterling's face. 'Four years,' he said after a moment, and his eyes were suddenly hard and contemptuous.

Danielle took a step backwards. She would have walked out of the office if Hugh had not said, 'The memos, Mr Tenassik . . .'

'The memos, yes. Sit down, please, Miss Payne.'

Somehow she found a chair. She sat on the edge of it, her back ramrod-stiff, her eyes firmly fixed on her notebook, where Sterling could not see them. He dictated a series of memos, and Danielle was not surprised that his style was quick, crisp and decisive. Charlie had been a ditherer, given to many ums and ers and masses of amendments; Sterling, on the other hand, was a man who would always know exactly what he wanted.

At last he was finished. Danielle glanced at him as she rose from her chair. His eyes met hers, and as one eyebrow lifted sardonically heat rushed into her cheeks.

Abruptly, she turned. The way from the chair to the door had never seemed quite so long; never before had there been the need to keep her shoulders so straight, to concentrate on setting one foot firmly and deliberately in front of the other.

Once outside the door, however, her shoulders drooped, and as she leaned against the wall her breathing came in heaving gasps. It was a minute or two before she felt able to go back to her desk.

'What's he like?'

Irene's desk was beside Danielle's. She was a pretty blonde girl who had recently become engaged.

'Like?' Danielle repeated dully.

'Mr Tenassik.'

'Oh, right. He... He...' She stopped.

'Is it true he's incredibly sexy?'

'He's good-looking.'

'A hunk?'

'I... I couldn't say...'

'Good grief, Danielle, you're the first to see him. You must be able to tell us something about him.'

'No.'

'The very least you can do is report back. Unless...' Irene's eyes were suddenly bright with interest. 'Something happened! He made a pass at you?'

'No!'

'Something did happen, I can tell,' Irene insisted.

Something had happened, of course. Something earth-shaking, momentous. Ten days of magic in Hawaii, a holiday Danielle would never forget. She had fallen crazily in love with Sterling, and had returned to California knowing that she would never love another man. None of which she would tell Irene.

'He didn't make a pass,' Danielle said. 'Look, I don't want to be rude, but I have a stack of memos to do. Better get started right away.'

Charlie Miller had always said that Danielle was the best secretary he had ever known. She was respected in the company for her accuracy and for the way in which her hands flew across the keyboard. Today, however, it was as if her fingers had turned into sausages, bumping clumsily into each other and hitting all the wrong keys; her shorthand symbols were a blur before her eyes.

Half an hour later, still busy with the first memo, she started when someone said, 'Danielle.'

Hugh Anderson was standing by her desk, looking down at her curiously. 'Are you going to tell me what that was all about?' he asked.

'I'm not sure what you mean,' Danielle said, to give herself time, although she knew perfectly well what Hugh was getting at.

'You and our new boss—have you met before?'

'Hugh...'

'You could have cut the atmosphere with a knife, it was so tense. You have met, haven't you?'

'Yes,' she whispered, relieved that Irene was temporarily away from her desk.

'I take it the encounter wasn't particularly pleasant?'

Danielle looked up at Hugh, her eyes clouded with unhappiness. 'I'd rather not talk about it.'

'I wouldn't pry if I didn't feel I had to.' Ordinarily, Hugh Anderson was the most pleasant of men, but there were times when he could be inflexible. 'The company is going through a period of reconstruction, as you well know, and things are tough enough without personality clashes in the office. Especially between a secretary and the new chief executive.'

She stared at him. 'Are you asking me to leave?'

For just a moment Hugh hesitated. 'No,' he said then, 'of course not; you're an excellent worker.'

'Then why all these questions?'

'I need to know that things will continue to function smoothly.'

'As butter,' Danielle answered with unaccustomed tartness.

Hugh reddened. 'Are you going to be able to work with Mr Tenassik?'

Danielle was already regretting her sarcasm. Hugh was only doing what he had to; it was not his fault that she and Sterling had struck sparks off each other.

'My job is important to me; I want to keep it,' she said quietly. 'I'll work with Sterling Tenassik—no need for you to worry about that.'

When she heard the chime of the clock in the reception area, Danielle took a breath. Noon, and time for lunch. Time, at last, for the thing she had been waiting most of the morning to do.

Outside Sterling's office she paused. Her instinct was to turn tail while she could still do so, but she knew it was impossible. She and Sterling had to talk.

The door was open and she walked right in. Only to stop quite still a second later.

Once more Sterling was standing by the window, but this time there was a woman with him—very close to him. Hair the colour of polished ebony was drawn back in a sleek chignon. A scarlet dress moulded a gorgeous, model-like figure. Her face was tilted upwards, her arms were around Sterling's neck; she seemed to be waiting for his kiss.

Danielle's gasp of pain was involuntary. Sterling's head turned. At sight of Danielle, standing ashen-faced in the doorway, a questioning eyebrow lifted.

'Can I help you?' he asked, his tone polite and a little amused.

At that moment, as if she realised that he had been distracted, the woman turned as well. Intent only on leaving the office as quickly as she could, Danielle caught no more than a very fleeting glimpse of huge dark eyes and a sensuously pouting mouth.

'Well?' Sterling asked.

Danielle did not answer him. In a minute she was back at her desk. Irene had already left the office to have lunch with her fiancé, and for that Danielle was grateful. As she sank into her chair, her body trembling, she wondered if it was really possible that a heart could break.

'Mommy!'

Danielle burst out laughing as Toby, a tiny human dynamo, came hurtling down the steps of the house towards her. It was the first time she had laughed that day.

Opening her arms to Toby, she hugged him tightly. His hair, only a little less downy than an infant's, was fragrant with the spicy smell of shampoo, and his little body was warm against her skin.

'Do you have to go to work tomorrow, Mommy?' he asked against her ear. He asked the same question at least three times every week.

'You know I do, Toby.'

'Can't you stay home with me?'

'No, honey, though I wish I could. Tell me what you did today.'

'Went to the park with Grandpa.'

'That must have been fun.'

'We didn't stay long; Grandpa was tired.'

The laughter stopped in Danielle's throat. Since his recent surgery her father was often tired. He adored Toby—both her parents did—but Danielle knew that keeping up with the demands of an energetic child was becoming a bit too much for them. Not that either of her parents would ever admit that this was so.

'Tell you what,' she said. 'How about you and I go to the park for a while before supper?'

'Yippee!' Toby shouted.

'I'll just go inside first and put on some other clothes and see if Gran can do with some help.'

Danielle's mother was in the kitchen preparing a salad. She smiled as Danielle dropped a kiss on her cheek.

No, she said in answer to her daughter's query, she needed no help. Supper was going to consist largely of leftovers from the previous day. And it would do Toby no end of good to work off some excess energy before bedtime.

When Danielle had changed from her sleek cream skirt and matching blouse into shorts and a T-shirt, she walked with Toby to the park. For more than half an hour they played together. Danielle was teaching Toby to catch a ball, and every day his skills were improving. When he grew bored with the ball, they went to the swings. The little boy loved the swings and kept begging his mother to push him higher. 'Higher, Mommy! Higher!' No wonder his grandfather was often tired.

The sun was setting when Danielle was at last able to coax Toby into going home.

As she had often of late, she took a detour, stopping in front of a house a few blocks away from her parents' home. The house was painted pink and it had a red roof and windows framed by black shutters. Dahlias and sweet peas grew profusely in the flowerbeds on either side of the house, and at one end of the garden were a few crab-apple trees. At the other end was a little play area with a swing and a sandpit. On the fence hung a 'FOR SALE' notice which Danielle had been eyeing for several weeks.

The house was quite small, yet more than big enough for a mother and one lively three-year-old. Danielle, who had gone to view it when it had been on show a week earlier, had only to close her eyes to picture its layout. It had captured her imagination the moment she had seen it.

'What's wrong, Mommy?'

Until Toby asked the question, Danielle was unaware that she had sighed.

'Nothing,' she said, reaching for the little boy's hand. 'Time to eat, honey. Let's go home.'

Toby was a darling, but there were times when he became very restless, and this particular evening was such a time. Perhaps the three adults had lingered too long over their meal, or perhaps it was just the natural capriciousness of a three-year-old asserting itself. For one reason or another, Toby began to knock his spoon rhythmically against his glass. No amount of coaxing on Danielle's part could persuade him to stop. And when she moved the glass out of his reach he drummed against a plate instead.

When Danielle's father put a hand against his temple, she knew that his head was beginning to ache. Her mother, always in tune with her husband's feelings, said, 'Toby, stop that noise.'

The little boy stuck out his bottom lip. A second later the knocking continued.

'Stop!' Danielle ordered.

'It's OK,' her gentle father protested.

'No,' Danielle said, 'it's not. Stop that noise right now, Toby. If you don't, you'll have to leave the table without any ice cream.'

For a few seconds there was silence and it appeared as if Danielle's threat had been effective. And then the knocking started once more, more softly this time yet just as annoying.

'Leave the room,' she ordered, but an unrepentant Toby only gave her a rebellious look.

At length Danielle had no choice but to lift him out of his chair and carry him out. At which point a squirming Toby burst into tears. 'Want my ice cream,' he wept.

'Not tonight,' Danielle told him quietly.

Half an hour later, after she had bathed a now subdued child and read him his customary bedtime stories, she rejoined her parents in the living-room.

'I'm sorry,' her father said when she sat down. 'I wish we hadn't been so impatient with Toby.'

'He has to learn, Dad.'

'It upsets me when he's unhappy.'

'And I'm upset when I see you looking tired and strained. You shouldn't have to put up with a small child. Not all day, anyway.' Danielle took a breath. 'You've been marvellous, both of you, letting me live with you when I needed help, looking after Toby all day while I work. But I've been thinking—it's time we had our own home.'

'Good heavens!' The exclamation came from her mother, but she saw both her parents looking at her in astonishment.

'I know just the place,' Danielle said.

She told them about the little house with the red roof and the apple trees and the swing.

'It's perfect,' she said. 'Problem is, it's only a dream at this point because I need more money. I've been saving every dollar I can, but it will still be a while before I have enough for a deposit, and by then the house will be gone. But I'll find something else.'

'You sound determined,' her mother said thoughtfully.

'I am. You shouldn't have to put up with the kind of turmoil Toby can create. As for Toby, he's just a little kid; he should be able to run and shout to his heart's content.' She pushed a restless hand through her hair. 'My savings are growing. Thanks to the two of you, I've been able to put away much of my earnings. But I still need quite a bit more if I'm going to have enough for a deposit on a house.'

Her father looked unhappy. 'We'd help you if we could.'

'I know that, Dad.' She went over to his chair and gave him a hug. 'But I need to do this on my own. I keep waiting for a decent raise.'

'Can't be long now, can it? You're so well thought of at the company.'

'I *was*.'

They were both looking at her uneasily now. 'What do you mean?' asked her mother after a moment.

'Things changed today. Radically,' Danielle said grimly. 'So much so that I think I may have to find myself another job.'

'You're kidding, Danielle!'

'I only wish I was. I love my job, and this morning I told Hugh Anderson that I meant to keep it. Since then I've had seconds thoughts.'

'Something's happened.' Her father was looking really worried now. 'What is it?'

They did not interrupt Danielle once as she proceeded to tell them about Sterling.

'Does he know you have a child?' her mother asked at length.

'No.'

An uneasy silence greeted her words. Danielle saw her parents exchange a quick glance, then they were both looking at her.

'Danielle...' her father said.

'Don't say it, Dad.'

'You'll be working with the man. This isn't a secret you can keep.'

'I have to. I intend to.'

Another quick glance. When her mother spoke again, her tone was uncertain. 'Maybe this isn't my business, but I feel I have to say it all the same—'

'Mom—'

'Shouldn't Sterling know the truth, Danielle? After all, he *is* Toby's father.'

CHAPTER TWO

'EARLY, aren't you, Danielle?'

The mug shook in her hand and a little coffee spilled onto the employment pages of the morning paper which she had spread in front of her on the desk.

Danielle had arrived at the office at seven rather than eight that morning, hoping that she could make some headway with her job search before the rest of the staff arrived. The office had been so still until this moment that she had been sure she was alone.

Only when she knew that she could face Sterling impassively did she look up. 'No rule against being early. At least there hasn't been until now—*Mr Tenassik*.'

Sterling's eyes glinted. 'Make a habit of being the first one in the office, do you?'

'Not as a rule. But why do you ask? Do you really care about the habits of the secretaries?'

'Let's just say that in your case I'm interested,' he said smoothly.

'I haven't breached security, and I'm not about to sell any company secrets. When did you get here, Sterling? Sorry, I mean Mr Tenassik . . .'

'Skip the sarcasm,' he said crisply.

'*You* set the tone when you insisted on calling me by my surname yesterday,' Danielle said heatedly. '*Miss Payne*, when you could so easily have called me Danielle.'

'I could, couldn't I?' If he was at all put out by the attack he did not show it.

'What are you doing here anyway?' Danielle continued. 'I thought there was no one about.'

'Like you, I arrived early. What were you busy with when I disturbed you?'

'As you see—drinking my coffee and reading the paper.'

'The want ads, by the look of it. Looking for another job, are you, Danielle?'

She hesitated a moment, then said, 'Maybe.'

'According to Hugh Anderson you're a whiz of a secretary and in line for a big raise. Which makes this a strange time to be looking for something new, doesn't it?'

A big raise. Danielle blinked back sudden tears as a vision of the red-roofed house passed briefly in front of her eyes. Sterling was right—talk about bad timing!

She swallowed hard. 'Not that strange.'

'Why, Danielle?'

'Does there have to be a reason?' she asked tersely.

She flinched when his hand went to her face, his thumb stroking the sensitive skin beneath her chin. Liquid fire raced through her body, reminding her of the magic they had once shared.

'There is a reason, and we both know it,' Sterling said mockingly. 'You can't bear to remain in this office now that I'm here.'

Unsteadily Danielle countered, 'Isn't it the other way around? *You* want *me* gone.'

'Is that what you think?'

'What do you expect me to think after the way you behaved yesterday? If you want me to resign—and why else would you be at my desk now?—I'm doing you a favour. I'm leaving without being asked.'

'I see,' Sterling said.

Heat rushed into Danielle's cheeks. More forcefully than was necessary, she pulled away from Sterling's hand. 'I'll give Hugh my notice the moment he gets in. I had intended working the usual two weeks but now I've changed my mind. If it's possible, if Hugh thinks he can make other arrangements, I'll leave today—tomorrow at the latest. I know *you* won't mind.'

How she would manage without a job heaven only knew. She would have to find a way, even if it meant using some of her precious savings to tide her over. But she would have to think about all that later.

Sterling was looking down at her, his dark eyes shuttered, so that Danielle could not read their expression.

'Strange,' he said at last. 'There was a time when I thought I knew you.'

Her eyes widened at the oddness of his tone. 'Sterling...?' she said uncertainly.

But he was talking again, as if he hadn't heard her. 'And then yesterday I walked into this company and found a girl who was so changed that I didn't know her at all.'

He was a right one to talk about change! There were things Danielle would have liked to say to Sterling—things she would have said to him yesterday if the ebony-haired woman had not been with him—and now she could not say them after all because she had an awful feeling that she might cry if she tried.

'Leave me alone,' was as much as she managed to whisper.

'In a moment. Hold the resignation until we've had a chance to talk.'

Hope flared inside her. With a tight throat she said, 'Talk about what—the office?'

He grinned at her. 'Of course. What else?'

She looked away from him, hiding her disappointment. 'OK, Sterling, what is it?'

'Later. We'll talk after work.'

'Whatever you have to say, I'd prefer you to say it now.'

'This evening, Danielle.'

'During the day or not at all.'

He lifted her left hand and looked at it. 'No ring; you're not married.'

She shook her head.

'So there's no husband you have to get home to.' He let the hand drop. 'A date?'

Danielle hesitated. 'Someone will be waiting for me,' she said at last.

There was the smallest quiver of movement in Sterling's jaw. Toby had that quiver too, usually when he was upset about something.

'Put him off.' The order was authoritative.

Danielle's head went up. 'Charlie Miller never expected his employees to give up their personal time. Not unless it was really important.'

'I'm not Charlie Miller,' came the crisp response.

Never a truer word spoken. Charlie had been a lamb: soft, sweet, malleable. This new Sterling was a lion of a man: strong, unexpectedly ruthless, the undisputed master of his domain. And, with it all, still the most attractive man Danielle had ever met, though now, four years later, he frightened her a little.

Yet, despite herself, Danielle was intrigued by his request. 'If I agree to meet you, it will have to be immediately after work.'

He gave a curt nod of assent. 'Fine.'

He was walking away from her desk when Danielle said, 'Sterling?' And when he turned she added, 'I can't be too long. The person I spoke of...he'll still be waiting for me when I get back.'

Sterling's expression was ominous, warning her that she was playing with fire. Danielle could not have him finding out about Toby; all the same, the knowledge that she had annoyed him gave her a moment of perverse satisfaction.

Danielle waited until the last person had left the office before she knocked on Sterling's door. The fact that she was meeting him after work would have occasioned gossip, especially among the secretaries, who, after just one day, were almost to a person star-struck over the new boss.

He looked up from his desk. 'I was beginning to wonder whether you'd come.'

'I told you I would.'

'So you did—under protest,' he said, with the unexpected smile that she remembered so well. It was a smile that warmed his eyes and tilted his lips; as always, it found its way straight to Danielle's heart. It even brought the beginnings of a smile to her own face.

And then Danielle remembered Sterling's behaviour a day earlier, and the beautiful, dark-haired woman, and the smile died on her lips.

'I hope this won't take long,' she said stiffly.

'Still have that other arrangement?'

'Very much so,' she responded tartly.

'Sit down, Danielle.'

She sat in the chair by the desk where she'd sat the previous day. Glancing at the man in the chair opposite her, she found herself having to push memories from her mind.

She sat up straight. 'What do you want of me, Sterling?'

'I have a proposition to put to you.'

'A proposition! You must be kidding! We've been through that before. The whole scene. Dining, dancing, swimming in the moonlight. Kissing—' She stopped, appalled that she had spoken without thinking.

'Making love,' Sterling said, and her head jerked upwards.

Making love... That was what it had been, at least for Danielle. For Sterling it had never been more than sex. The ten days in Hawaii had been nothing but a holiday romance: enjoyable while the holiday lasted, intended to be forgotten the moment it came to an end.

'If you're thinking of a repetition, it's not on,' she said flatly.

'Sure of that, Danielle?' he drawled.

'So sure that there's nothing to talk about. You wasted my time and your own by asking me to come here. Goodnight, Sterling.' She rose from her chair.

'Not so fast, Danielle.'

'I've already told you that I won't—'

'It's not that kind of proposition.'

Danielle saw the mocking gleam in Sterling's eyes, and in a moment she understood that by jumping to conclusions she had made a fool of herself. Her cheeks flooded with sudden colour.

'I think I should go,' she said unsteadily.

'Not before we've talked.'

'We have nothing to talk about.'

'Don't we? I remember how we used to talk. Every night. When we weren't kissing—and that took up much of our time, didn't it?—we were talking. Sometimes we talked for so long that the dawn would creep up on us without us noticing it. There was so much to talk about, Danielle.'

Except for a few really important things, and they had deliberately shied clear of those topics.

'We had a lot in common—then,' she said slowly, sinking back down into the chair.

'*Then*, Danielle?'

'You know exactly what I mean. And by the way, what was it all about yesterday, Sterling? You still haven't said. *Miss Payne*, spoken so coldly. The outstretched hand. Pretending we'd never met. I took my cue from you; it was obvious that was what you wanted. But you're mistaken if you think Hugh was fooled. He caught the tension; he asked me afterwards if we'd met before. I didn't give him a proper answer, but I didn't have to; Hugh isn't stupid.'

'I wasn't expecting you to walk through that door, Danielle. The name Payne meant nothing to me. You caught me off guard.'

'Do you think *I* wasn't shocked? The name Tenassik didn't set bells ringing in my mind either; I had no idea you were the new chief executive. But shock doesn't even begin to explain the way you behaved—the formality, the hostility. We didn't part on bad terms, Sterling.'

'We didn't part at all,' he said very coldly.

'What...what are you saying?' Danielle asked when she could trust herself to speak.

'You ran out on me. We'd made love the previous evening—in case you've forgotten—and when I woke up the next morning the bed was empty. I thought you'd gone to your hotel, that you were changing your clothes, that you'd be there waiting for me when I came to take you out for breakfast. Can you imagine my shock when I learned you'd gone? Without a single word. Without so much as saying goodbye.'

'Sterling—' She stopped, at a loss for the right words— because it was impossible to tell him the truth.

'Don't try telling me you've forgotten,' he said harshly.

'No...I haven't,' she said weakly.

She had forgotten nothing. Every detail of their time together was vividly raw in her memory, as if the events had taken place only yesterday...

It was the first day of her long-awaited holiday in Hawaii. A gorgeous day. The sun shone in a cloudless sky, the sea was a deep blue broken by the white crests of the incoming tide. Gulls soared in the air and swooped down low over the water, and the sound of the waves was a ceaseless roar.

Danielle stretched her long, slim limbs luxuriously, cat-like on the soft golden sand. Ten days lay ahead of her, with nothing to do but sleep and swim and sunbathe. Ten days of perfect relaxation with no thought of her life back in the United States, and certainly no thought of John—traitorous John who had so ruthlessly ended their engagement when a richer girl had come along.

She rummaged in her bag for her book, but she hadn't read more than three pages when the combination of the sun and the sound of the waves caused her eyes to close.

She woke up suddenly, jerking upright with a gasp of shock when the water hit her. It was a moment or two before she realised that a wave had washed over her. And then she was scrambling to her feet, frantic to snatch her possessions from the grip of the incoming tide. In dismay she saw her new sunhat, with its bright scarlet ribbon, being swept quickly down the wet sand towards the sea.

She was running towards the hat when a pair of big, tanned hands caught it. And then those same hands were helping Danielle to gather her things out of reach of the next wave.

'Safe and sound, though a bit wet.' The owner of the hands was laughing down at her from a spot higher up on the beach.

'Wet doesn't bother me,' Danielle laughed back at him. 'Nothing there that won't dry. Thanks for rescuing my hat; another second and it would have been food for the fish.'

'Guess you didn't realise the tide was coming in?'

'Guess not. I must have fallen asleep, because the last I remember is that the waves were still some way out.'

'The tide comes in quickly here, but perhaps you didn't know.'

'I didn't; it's my first day. I can't believe I slept so long.'

'Not all that long,' he drawled.

She tilted her head back to look at him. She had to tilt it quite far, Danielle realised. The man was very tall— taller than John; he was at least six feet two. His wind-blown hair was dark, his face attractively rugged.

Curiously she said. 'How would you know how long I slept?'

He laughed again, the sound vital and appealing against the roar of the waves. 'I was watching you.'

He had been watching her... For some reason the thought was unsettling.

'In that case,' Danielle said lightly, 'I wonder why you didn't wake me before the tide got to me?'

His eyes sparkled; he did not look at all abashed. 'Put it down to the fact that the wave that caught you was bigger than the rest. Still, I owe you an apology. Your towel is soaked, and, since it's all my fault, come and share mine.'

Danielle looked for a moment or two at the tall, very attractive man. 'I don't think so, but thanks anyway,' she said.

'Please.'

'It's not far to my hotel; I can easily get another towel.'

'Is that a high horse you've mounted?'

'Of course not.' Danielle couldn't help laughing. 'I wouldn't know a high horse if I saw one.'

The gaze that held hers was disturbingly male. 'That's a relief. Still, I won't consider myself truly forgiven unless you agree to my offer.'

Somewhere deep inside her a voice urged Danielle to persist in her refusal. Though the memory of John's betrayal was not nearly as painful as it had been—making her wonder whether she had ever loved him—she was reluctant to become involved with someone new.

'It's a big towel,' the man said.

'Are you always so persuasive?'

Again that attractive laugh. 'Persuasive? I hope so. Thing is, I can't have my conscience keeping me awake all night.'

Green eyes almost the colour of jade smiled up at him. 'All night? I don't believe your conscience would keep you awake for a minute. But, since you're so insistent, I'll share a bit of your towel—just until my own is dry, of course.'

She watched him shake the sand from his towel before spreading it once more over the sand. Already starting to regret her decision, Danielle was careful to place herself on one corner. To her dismay, the towel's owner chose to disregard the hint to seat himself on another corner and sat down a little too close to her instead.

'Not that bad, is it?' he asked with a grin, and she knew that her expression had given her away.

'I'm Sterling,' he told her.

'And I'm Danielle.' She introduced herself somewhat mechanically because on one level of her mind she was noticing every detail of the man whose body was just inches from her own.

Everything about Sterling was inordinately attractive: the broad shoulders and the muscled chest, the rugged face with its striking planes and angles, the laughter-lines creasing the skin around eyes that were as dark as his hair and flecked with gold, and the lips that were a tantalising mixture of strength and sensuousness. He had the look of a man who had seen something of life, Danielle thought. She placed him in his early thirties.

As he shifted his position on the towel, one of his legs touched hers. Involuntarily Danielle shivered. In a moment she was on her feet.

'Hey,' Sterling said. 'Aren't you forgetting your towel is wet?'

'It's fine,' she said lightly.

'It's wet through.'

'It's not that bad. Look, I appreciate your help, but I really must be getting back to the hotel.'

'The high horse again.'

'I told you,' she said, but brittly this time, 'I wouldn't recognise one if we met.'

'Why don't I believe you?'

'I've no idea.'

'Have dinner with me tonight, Danielle.'

'Thanks, but I don't think so.' The words emerged a little too quickly.

'Another date?'

'Not exactly...'

'I hope you're not going to tell me you have letters to write. Or, horror of horrors, that you intend to spend the evening washing your hair. It looks wonderful just as it is.'

It was hard not to smile at him. 'You seem to know all the lines,' Danielle said, doubting if the woman lived who would have the will-power to resist this man for very long.

'Every one,' he assured her solemnly. 'So there's no point in trying them. You will come, won't you, Danielle?'

She was still hesitating when he added, 'I take you for a girl who likes a good lobster. I know a wonderful restaurant. It's built high on a cliff and you can watch the waves crashing on the rocks while you dine on the best seafood in the world. Meet you in the foyer of your hotel at eight?'

Throwing caution to the wind, Danielle could only nod her assent.

Sterling was waiting for her when she emerged from the lift a few hours later. His back was to her, but his height and the breadth of his shoulders told her that it had to be him. He must have sensed her presence, for he turned suddenly, smiling when he saw her, and the breath caught in her throat. He wore a navy jacket with an open-necked shirt and cream-coloured trousers, and even with clothes covering the superb body he was striking.

'You look beautiful,' he said, and suddenly Danielle was glad that she had chosen one of her favourite dresses—sleeveless, with a scooped neckline and a skirt that flowed softly from a tiny, belted waist. The line of the dress flattered her slender figure and its colour was almost exactly the same shade as her eyes. 'Very beautiful,' he said softly, and, as before, it was impossible not to smile back at him.

The restaurant to which he took her was every bit as appealing as he'd promised. What he'd neglected to mention was that it was almost unbearably romantic.

When the waiter had taken their order—lobster thermidor for two—Danielle looked at Sterling. 'There's something I need to say.'

'Say away.'

'I...I hope you won't be offended.'

The eyes that rested on hers were curious. 'Try me.'

'I—' Danielle stopped.

'Why don't you just say it?' Sterling suggested easily.

The words emerged in a rush. 'I need to keep things light between us.'

After what seemed like an awfully long moment, Sterling said, 'I see.'

'You probably think I'm being presumptuous... I mean, I know this is just a very casual dinner, that we might never see each other again after tonight... probably won't—'

'Probably will. At least, if I have my way. I hope that we *will* see each other again, Danielle. Any particular reason why we shouldn't?'

'Not exactly.' She moved restlessly in her seat.

'Let's see; you're married and you just forgot to wear your ring today?'

'It's not that.'

'Engaged? Fiancé lurking behind the palm trees, waiting to knock off my head when we leave the restaurant?'

She couldn't help smiling at his nonsense. 'Don't be silly.'

'Well, then?'

Sterling was right: it would be best to say what she had to and get it over with quickly. After that she would be able to relax and enjoy the evening.

'No surnames,' she said. 'I'm Danielle, you're Sterling; it's as much as either of us need to know.'

The eyes on her face were disturbing. 'A woman of mystery and determined to remain one. You intrigue me, Danielle.'

'There's really no mystery.' She tried to force a smile. 'I'm not in hiding, and I'm not on the run because of some awful crime.'

'I know that,' he said with a sureness that surprised her. 'But there has to be a reason all the same.'

She took a breath. 'There is. I've just come out of something a bit...a bit unpleasant. I'm not ready for anything new. That's why...I don't suppose you can understand; you must think I'm crazy.'

The dark eyes held hers for what seemed like eternity. Danielle wished she knew what Sterling was thinking. Far below them a wave rose, crested, broke on jagged rocks with a deafening roar. A seagull, still searching for fish, hovered over the water.

'You're not crazy,' Sterling said at last. 'And I do understand.'

'You do?'

'No surnames—that's a condition I can live with.'

Danielle sat back in her seat. 'Good.'

'I approve of your terms.'

'Really?'

'They happen to suit me too.'

'Great,' Danielle said after a moment.

'In fact,' Sterling said, 'we can take this thing a step further. No exchanging addresses.'

'Two anonymous people.'

'Enjoying each other's company while the holiday lasts. No lingering farewells when it ends. No regrets or reproaches. No strings attached.'

'A holiday friendship.' Danielle wondered why her lightness was quite so forced. Sterling's terms were exactly what she wanted—weren't they?

'That's settled, then.'

'You've had a bad experience too, haven't you?' Danielle said slowly. 'You're just as reluctant to get involved with anyone as I am.'

'Most people have a past,' Sterling answered her noncommittally. His eyes took on a sudden sparkle. 'Here comes our waiter with the lobster. Just as well we got the serious talking over first; now we can really enjoy our dinner.'

For two people who had set conditions to their relationship, they talked with all the ease of old friends. They had much in common; they had differences as well. They liked the same books and music, they both adored horses, but Sterling enjoyed hunting while Danielle hated blood sports with a passion. On this topic they agreed to disagree. Hours passed, and when the lights in the restaurant dimmed Danielle was surprised to realise that traitorous John had not appeared in her mind even once all evening.

They were about to leave the table when Sterling said, 'You're quite a girl, Danielle.'

She stiffened.

He must have seen her reaction. 'Anything wrong with me saying that? After all, we both know where we stand.' Leaning forward, he reached for her hands. 'Ten days, beautiful Danielle. A holiday friendship with no strings attached and no regrets at the end of it. Let's make the most of it while it lasts.'

His hands were as big as the rest of him. They folded over her small ones, covering every inch of skin. Warm hands, sending the blood racing through Danielle's veins all the way up her arms to her shoulders.

Briefly, she wondered whether it was possible to have a mere friendship with this man. Could she see him day after day without falling in love with him? Of course she could—and would, she told herself firmly.

Four years later, facing him across the wide expanse of desk in an office in San Francisco, Danielle wondered how she could have been so confident—and so stupid.

'So you haven't forgotten.' His eyes were hard, the line of his jaw inflexible.

'Why would I?'

She heard the hiss of his breath. 'You're very cool, aren't you, Danielle? That's something I never realised about you in Hawaii.'

She made herself sit very still. 'Why do you say that?'

'It's as if the time we spent together meant nothing to you.'

'That's not true at all; we had a wonderful time.' She tried to speak lightly over the tears that threatened to close her throat.

'So wonderful that you ran away without a backward glance when it was over.'

Danielle lifted her head. 'That's not fair, Sterling. I kept to our terms.'

'What the hell are you saying?'

'Perhaps *you've* forgotten. First names only. No exchange of addresses. No lingering farewells, no strings attached.'

He took a step towards her, and she saw that his face had gone very pale. 'You're throwing that at me?'

'Just repeating our agreement.'

'An agreement made the first evening, before we got to know each other, by a girl and a guy who shared a dry towel, and then went out for dinner together.'

'Are you saying that things changed?' Danielle asked tensely.

Sterling was quiet for so long that Danielle wondered if he meant to speak at all. 'Maybe not,' he said at last. His expression was unreadable.

'In other words, there was nothing wrong about my leaving the way I did.' Tears pricked her eyelids. 'I don't understand your hostility, Sterling. I'd have thought you'd be glad that I spared us both the trauma of a lingering farewell. It was the one thing we both dreaded.'

Sterling looked at her with hooded eyes. After a moment Danielle rose abruptly from her chair. She had to get out of his office: she could keep the tears at bay for only so long and she did not want him to see them.

'Wait!' Sterling ordered as she made for the door.

Danielle shook her head. 'There's nothing more to say.'

'There is. You forget, I had a purpose in asking you here.'

'You wanted to accuse me of being a cold, unfeeling bitch. What else can there possibly be, Sterling?'

'There was something more.'

'What?'

'The reason I asked you here in the first place.'

Amazingly, it had not taken him long to regain his composure. He was standing now with his back against the desk, one long leg leaning across the other—a man totally in command of himself.

'It's getting late; I told you someone's waiting for me.'

'Sit,' he said, as if he had not heard her.

'I don't think so.'

'This won't take long.'

Lips tight, Danielle returned to the desk and sank back into her chair. 'What is it, Sterling?' she asked.

For another long, infuriating moment he looked at her. Then he said, quite calmly, 'I want you to be my private secretary.'

CHAPTER THREE

DANIELLE stared at Sterling in amazement. A moment or two passed before she answered him. 'I don't believe you just said that.'

His eyes glinted with the laughter she remembered. 'Why not?'

'We've been at arm's length since the moment we set eyes on each other yesterday.'

'May I remind you that Hugh Anderson has a high opinion of you?'

'I happen to know that you don't give a fig for Hugh's opinions.'

'Why wouldn't I?'

'Because you make up your own mind about things; you don't let other people sway you.'

Once more that glint. 'You seem to know a lot about me, Danielle.'

'Of course; all the staff do. Your reputation preceded you, Sterling. You're the high-powered chief executive who will come in and set the company on its head, after which nothing will ever be quite the same again.'

'Is that what you heard?'

Infuriatingly, the laughter had not left his face. Danielle wondered what it would take to get through to him.

'There was more,' she said deliberately.

'Let me guess. I frighten the life out of secretaries who can't spell. I haunt their dreams if they make mistakes with my appointments. I make life generally unpleasant for anyone who works for me.'

'You have some of it right,' she said noncommittally.

The fact was that men spoke of Sterling Tenassik as a person who was something of a miracle man: a financial wizard who could take an ailing company and turn it into a thriving gold-mine. Women, while appreciating that asset as well, also raved about his looks, personality and sexiness.

'Why do you want me to be your personal secretary, Sterling?'

'You're the right person.'

Danielle had long wanted to make progress in her career. With Toby's arrival she had had to abandon her cherished plans to study art; instead she had taken a clerical position with the advertising company. Little by little, she had found herself growing more and more interested in the industry. She loved to look at layouts that other people had created and think about the approach she herself would have taken.

On one memorable occasion an idea she had suggested to Charlie Miller had actually been adopted, and she had had the thrill of being allowed to work on its implementation. She dreamed of taking courses and extending her knowledge. As the personal secretary of the company's chief executive, she would, willy-nilly, learn more about advertising. If only the new president were anyone other than Sterling...

'Some of the others would do just as well as me,' she said.

'As far as I'm concerned, you're the one I want.' There was such an odd note in his tone.

Trying to ignore the shiver that slid down her spine, Danielle said, 'We've always worked in a typing pool until now; I told you that yesterday. Even Charlie used the pool.'

'My style is different. I prefer to have my own secretary.'

'I'll have to think about it, Sterling.'

'There's something else you should think about at the same time. As my secretary, you'll have to do some travelling.'

'Travelling?' Danielle asked in surprise.

Sterling's eyes held hers. 'With me.'

In a second Danielle's pulses were racing. And then she looked into Sterling's face—the *new* Sterling, who was so different from the man she had fallen in love with four years earlier—and her pulse rate slowly returned to normal.

'What exactly do you mean?' she asked in a strained voice.

'I do a fair amount of travelling. As my secretary, you'd be expected to accompany me.'

'I take it,' she said carefully, 'that you're talking of day trips.'

'No.'

'You can't—' she swallowed '—mean I'd have to spend any nights away from home.'

'That is exactly what I mean,' Sterling answered her deliberately and with evident satisfaction.

A shudder went through her. 'Charlie Miller didn't travel.'

'When will you understand that I'm not Charlie? There's a trip in the works right now, Danielle. An important one. If it's successful, it could mean prosperity for the company. I want you to come with me.'

Danielle made herself ask the question. 'Won't your wife mind?'

'I'm not married.'

Happiness exploded inside her—an irrational happiness, considering that whatever there had once been between Sterling and her had ceased to exist long ago.

'Oh...I thought maybe...'

'What did you think, Danielle?' he asked softly.

She looked at him, then away. 'It doesn't matter.'

'I'd like to hear it all the same.'

She had begun to tremble; it was only with a great effort of will that she forced herself not to let him see it. Somehow she managed to meet a gaze that was both mocking and disturbing. 'You were with a woman yesterday. I thought she might be your wife.'

'She is not,' Sterling said pleasantly.

Danielle waited a moment. Girlfriend? Fiancée? What was the role of the dark-haired woman in Sterling's life? But Sterling did not elaborate.

Instead he said, 'Do I have a secretary?'

'No.'

'Why not?'

'I don't think it's a good idea.'

'Why is that?'

'It wouldn't work. You and I . . .' She shook her head a little too violently. 'No, Sterling.'

'It worked once before.'

Within seconds a flush had risen in her cheeks. 'This is different. Don't you see? Don't go on with this, Sterling; there's no point. I've made up my mind.'

She glanced at her watch. Toby would have had his bath by now; he might even have had his supper. But he would be awake still, and getting impatient, waiting for her to read him his stories.

'I have to go,' she said.

'That person you mentioned—do you think he's still waiting?'

She met his eyes levelly. 'I'm quite sure he is.'

'He'll object if you're late?'

'He won't be at all happy.'

She was about to stand once more when Sterling said, 'We haven't spoken about money. How much are you earning now, Danielle?'

'It's irrelevant.'

'Is it?'

'Of course.'

'How much, Danielle?'

'Hugh Anderson will tell you how much I earn if you really want to know.'

'I'm asking *you*, Danielle.'

She hesitated a few seconds. Then, realising that there was no point in hiding from Sterling something that he could find out quite easily without her help, she told him what he wanted to know. 'And this morning you mentioned a raise,' she added.

Sterling was silent for a while. At length he said, 'Be my secretary; travel with me...and I'll double that amount, and that includes the raise.'

Danielle stared at him disbelievingly. *Double her salary!* With what she had saved already she might soon have enough for the deposit on a house—the red-roofed house if she was really lucky.

She was unaware of the sudden radiance in her face: her eyes shone like polished jewels and her cheeks glowed with colour.

'Make a difference?' Sterling's tone was friendly.

'Maybe.'

'Enough to get you to change your mind?'

Danielle hesitated. There was Toby. He was extremely attached to his grandparents and they loved him so dearly that she was almost sure that they would not mind taking sole responsibility for him for a little while. Yet she *hated* the idea of being apart from her child, even for a few days. Balanced against that was the prospect of a house, and every day it became clearer how important it was that she make a home for Toby and herself—for all their sakes.

'Yes,' she said, a little breathlessly. 'Yes, I think so.'

'Let's get this straight.' He still spoke in the same friendly tone. 'You're agreeing to be my personal secretary?'

'I've just said so.'

'And you'll travel with me?'

Again she hesitated. 'If I have to.'

Silence followed Danielle's words. An odd silence, strangely charged, filling the office. Without knowing quite why, Danielle began to tremble.

'You've changed your mind,' she said at length, when Sterling still had not spoken. 'You don't want me after all.'

'I want you, Danielle. I've wanted you from the moment I first saw you,' he said deliberately.

Danielle felt another shiver deep inside her. When she had herself under control, she asked, 'What is it, then? There *is* something, I can tell.'

'I'm just wondering at the speed with which you changed your mind.' All pretence at friendliness was gone now; there was just Sterling's hard voice, mocking her, lashing her.

'What do you mean?' she whispered.

'I thought I knew you, Danielle—at least in some ways, because I came to realise that there were ways in which I didn't know you at all.' There was a pause before he continued. 'Fact is, I took you for a girl who would never do anything for a price.'

'What are you saying?'

'Only that it's interesting to discover that you have a price tag after all.'

Danielle froze on her chair. As the blood drained from her cheeks, her face went pale. For a few seconds all she could do was stare in shock at the man not two feet away from her.

Movement returned suddenly to her limbs. She did not look at Sterling as she jumped from her chair and made for the door, and he did not say a word to detain her.

The next morning she was again in the office early. This time she did not have the employment pages spread out in front of her. Nor did she bother to check whether Sterling had come to the office before her. When she had typed out her notice, she turned her attention to her desk. She would walk out the moment she had tidied her drawers, gathered her personal possessions and spoken to Hugh.

She was tugging things from a drawer when a long shadow fell across the early-morning rays of sun slanting through the east-facing window.

'Early again, Danielle?'

She did not lift her head. 'As you see.'

'What are you doing?'

'What does it look like?' she muttered tersely.

'Does Hugh know you're leaving?'

So he did not need an explanation, but then Sterling was nobody's fool.

'He doesn't know yet; he'll find out when he gets here. I should have finished emptying my desk by then. I'll say my goodbyes to Hugh and the staff, and then I'll go.'

Sterling was silent. Danielle wished he would leave her alone. It disturbed her profoundly to know that he was watching her.

She had emptied one drawer and was starting on the next when he said, 'Touched a raw nerve, did I?' Unexpectedly, his tone was gentle.

Hands that were busy putting loose paper-clips in a tray grew still.

'Danielle?'

'Yes,' she said in a low voice. 'You did.'

'I'm sorry.'

Danielle swallowed hard. After a moment she went on tidying the paper-clips.

She flinched when long fingers slid beneath the heavy fall of her hair, coming to rest on the back of her neck. 'Don't!' she grated. And when the fingers remained where they were she added, 'You could get into trouble, Sterling—don't you know that? Sexual harassment is a serious offence.'

His laughter was low and vibrant and unbearably seductive. 'We both know that's not what this is. From the start we could never get enough of each other. One kiss was always the prelude to the next. Don't you remember, Danielle?'

'I don't care to remember,' she whispered.

'Don't you? Well, let me tell you what you've forgotten—*if* you have, in fact, forgotten. The sparks were there from the moment we met. What existed between us was mutual; it was never harassment.'

'Not then,' she conceded painfully.

'Not now either.' As the fingers moved on her neck Danielle had to suppress another shiver. 'I told you I was sorry,' Sterling said.

'I heard you the first time, but I thought I must be imagining the words.'

'Do you want me to beg?'

'That would be a nice sight,' she muttered. 'The great chief executive on his knees in front of my desk. But don't bother. Just leave me alone—it's all I ask, Sterling, and I'll accept the apology as is.'

'I'll leave when I've confirmed your answer is still the same.'

This time Danielle's head went up. 'What are you talking about now?'

'Yesterday, before your hasty departure from my office, you agreed to be my personal secretary.'

Danielle stared at him, outraged. 'That was before you insulted me. You must be crazy if you think what I said yesterday means anything now.'

'You were willing to accompany me on my travels.' It was as if he hadn't heard her.

Once more Danielle thought of Toby, and of how much it would upset her not to see him even for a day. 'Actually,' she muttered, 'what I said was that I'd travel with you *if I had to*.'

Sterling grinned at her. 'Isn't that the same thing?'

'No.'

His eyes gleamed. 'Without debating the exact meaning of your words, did you mean that you'd come with me?'

'I meant it then.' She glared at him. 'For a few seconds. Until you made that vile crack about the price tag.'

'I've apologised for that.'

'And because I want to see the back of you I've accepted the apology. That doesn't mean I've forgotten what you said—or forgiven it.'

'Are you saying you've changed your mind?'

'Your arrogance did it for me. Find yourself another secretary, Sterling.'

'I want *you*, Danielle.'

'Impossible!'

'Even if I double the amount?'

She stared at him, green eyes dazed. 'What...what are you trying to do to me, Sterling?'

'I'll give you twice the amount I mentioned yesterday.'

'But that's exorbitant!' Danielle burst out. 'Far beyond any reasonable secretarial salary.'

'I'll pay it all the same.'

She shook her head. 'That kind of money... How can it be worth it to you?'

'It is.'

Excitement and nervousness warred in Danielle's head. 'Why?' she asked at last.

'I have my reasons.'

'What reasons, Sterling?' And when he did not speak she said, 'I have to know.'

Unmoved by her plea, Sterling remained silent. His eyes held hers, defying them to move away.

'Triple the amount,' he said at last. 'My final offer.'

'Sterling...' She was trembling visibly now; she knew he must see it.

'What do you say, Danielle?'

She wondered if he had any idea what he was offering her. Not only would she be able to pay the deposit on the house, but she would also have enough left over with which to turn it into a cosy home for herself and Toby. *Their son.*

'*If* I were to accept,' she said unsteadily, 'would you go on taunting me about my price? I couldn't bear it if you did.'

'You know that I've apologised for that.'

'Yes . . .'

'Well, Danielle?'

She wanted to hurl the offer in his face. Yet it was so tempting—she would be able to do so much for her family.

'Why me?' she asked, her voice low.

'You've already asked me that.'

'You didn't give me a satisfactory answer.'

'I can't give you a better one—for the moment.'

'For the moment?' she asked tensely.

But Sterling only looked at her, his expression enigmatic.

Danielle picked up a few more paper-clips. When she had dropped them in the tray she lifted her head once more. 'I'll have to think about it.'

'You surprise me.'

'I have to think all the same. It's not possible to give you an answer today.'

She held her breath as she awaited his answer.

'I'll expect to hear from you first thing tomorrow morning,' Sterling told her crisply. 'No later than nine-thirty.'

Toby seemed to sense that something was different that night. He found every excuse not to go to bed, and when he did put his head on the pillow at last, after three stories and a whole concert of songs, he found one pretext after another to call his mother back into his room. Eventually, however, fatigue got the better of him and he fell asleep.

Danielle made a big pot of tea and carried it into the living-room, where her parents were sitting in front of the TV. The show they were watching was just ending, and Danielle's father switched off the TV as she poured the tea.

'Toby asleep?' asked her mother.

'At last.' She gave them their tea, then settled herself in the rattan chair that had been her favourite since she'd been a child. 'We have to talk,' she said bleakly.

Her mother gave her a worried look. 'Sterling again?'

'Yes.' Danielle took a breath, then began to tell her parents her most recent news. They did not interrupt her once while she spoke, but their expressions revealed anxiety, surprise and shock.

'I have to give him an answer tomorrow morning,' Danielle said at length.

Her parents exchanged a quick look. After almost thirty years of marriage, they were often able to communicate without words.

'What will you tell him?' her father asked.

'That rather depends on you.' Danielle hesitated. 'You see, if I decide to accept Sterling's offer, it means leaving Toby with you.'

'No problem there. It's not as if we're not used to being with the boy. We love him dearly, and your mother and I look after him when you're at work anyway.'

'This is different. There'd be evenings when I wouldn't come home. You'd have to do everything for him.'

'We'd manage.'

'It might not be a matter of two or three days, Dad. Sterling didn't say how long we'd be away.'

Her parents were clearly taken aback, but after a few seconds Danielle's father said again, 'We'd manage. We would, wouldn't we, Anne?'

Danielle turned to her usually exuberant mother, who had remained curiously silent throughout the conversation. 'You haven't said anything, Mom.'

'Your dad's right—we'd manage,' her mother said, but slowly. 'Of course we would.'

'But you're not happy about it. Something's bothering you, Mom.'

Her mother's eyes were troubled. 'Toby's no problem; you know we adore him. It's Sterling, Danielle. If this new boss of yours were anyone but Sterling, I'd be as enthusiastic as your dad. As it is, I can't forget that he made you very unhappy.'

'Because of him I have Toby.'

'That isn't the point, honey. What happened once can happen again.'

'No, because this time I can trust myself,' Danielle said, with a conviction she was far from feeling. 'I'd make quite sure nothing happened. You forget, I'm twenty-three—almost four years older than I was in Hawaii, and a lot tougher. I can take care of myself, Mom. I wouldn't let Sterling get to me.'

Her mother poured herself more tea, then put down the cup without drinking. 'Easy to talk this way now, Danielle, more difficult when you're alone with him and your emotions are involved.'

'Not all that difficult, actually. Sterling isn't interested in me any longer. Not in that way...' Danielle swallowed hard, then went on. 'He's changed so much, I barely know him. And besides . . .' She paused again, then continued with a lightness which she hoped hid her pain, 'There's another woman in his life now. Seductive, glamorous—you should see her. I wouldn't be surprised if she's a model. He wouldn't be interested in me.'

'Well, then,' her father said gruffly, 'seems there isn't a problem after all. If you want to be Sterling's secretary and go on those trips, tell the man it's OK.'

'He'll break your heart—if you fall in love with him again,' said her mother.

Danielle looked away. It wasn't a question of falling in love with Sterling: she had never stopped loving him. Seeing him had made one thing crystal-clear: she loved him as much as ever.

'I think I have to do it all the same,' she said after a few moments.

'Danielle . . .' Her mother made one more try.

But Danielle shook her head. 'For all our sakes. Yours, Toby's and mine. Our own home. I may never have the chance to earn that much again.'

Her mother turned to her later, when they were tidying the kitchen. 'Will you tell Sterling about Toby?'

'Not that Toby is his son,' Danielle replied without hesitation. 'How can I, when he made it clear from the start that there could be no long-term commitment? He'd be *horrified* to learn he was a father.'

'You won't tell him anything?' her mother persisted.

Danielle's eyes were troubled. 'I think he does have to know that I have a child.'

Next day, on the dot of nine-thirty, Danielle told Sterling her decision. The eyes that flicked across her face gave nothing away, but all the same she had the feeling that he was not in the least surprised.

'You were expecting me to say yes,' Danielle said grimly.

'I thought you might.'

'Just don't hand me any more nasty cracks.'

'I told you I wouldn't.' Sterling was studying her, his expression almost uncannily like that of his son at certain times.

Restlessly, Danielle looked away from him. 'You haven't told me anything about my duties.'

'I haven't, have I?'

Her eyes returned to him. 'Secretarial, obviously.'

'Amongst other things.'

'Other things? What other things, Sterling? I need to know.'

'Social duties,' he told her.

She could not have explained her moment of apprehension. 'Social duties?' she repeated carefully.

'We'll be spending most of our time with other people. A couple, actually—a man and a woman. The man is a powerhouse in several industries, and I'm banking on an important account coming our way.'

'And the woman?'

'The woman—' Sterling's eyes gleamed '—is his wife.'

'I don't understand where I fit in,' Danielle said a little uncertainly. 'Are you expecting me to act as some kind of hostess?'

'Where we're going, they will be the hosts. You'll learn more about your duties as we go along, Danielle; no reason to worry about them now. What you do need to think about is some new clothes.'

'I have clothes.'

'Not the right ones, unless I'm mistaken.'

Danielle's face flushed with anger. 'Nobody in this office has ever complained about my appearance.'

'I'm not complaining either; you look just fine. But I'm not talking about office clothes. You'll be needing some special things for where we're going. Take a few days off—I'll clear it with Hugh—and go shopping. Look for casual things. Some swimwear. Dresses and trousers for the evening.'

She tried to control a sudden trembling. 'The way you're talking, you make it sound as if we'll be away quite some time.'

'I can't tell you how long it will be.'

This was a lot worse than she had realised. *Toby,* she thought. 'I need to know...'

'But I can't tell you. By the way, Danielle, money is of no account. Just make certain that whatever you get is the best.'

Hiding her nervousness, she managed some flippancy. 'I might just decide to buy out San Francisco.'

But it was hard to shake a laughing Sterling. 'Get what you have to. One proviso—I want to see everything that you buy.'

'You need to give your stamp of approval?'

'Precisely.'

She stared at him. 'Why am I beginning to feel like some kind of high-class call-girl?'

'I've no idea. What do you think?'

'Perhaps because all this talk about expensive clothes is making me feel uncomfortable.'

'Poor Danielle,' Sterling mocked.

'I think you should tell me more about this trip.'

'You'll find out all you need to know in due course.'

Danielle stood up. 'And I think I should back out right now.'

'That's up to you.'

'It is, isn't it?'

She was at the door when he said her name. 'Danielle?'

'Yes?'

'The money no longer means anything to you?'

She took a deep breath, her legs feeling suddenly weak. They gazed at each other across the room, Danielle hating Sterling for the hold he had over her.

Slowly, she came back to the desk. 'It means a lot,' she said bitterly.

'In that case,' Sterling said evenly, 'do your shopping. Just remember, I want to see all your purchases.'

Danielle's hands gripped the edge of the desk. There was something she had to say, but the words emerged with difficulty.

'This place you're taking me to...'

'Yes?' It was asked so politely.

'I won't have sex with you.'

Sterling's eyes gleamed. 'I don't remember inviting you to.'

Memories flooded her mind, unwanted and unbidden. Danielle was appalled at the rush of desire that swept through her, at the urgent need to fling herself into Sterling's arms, to feel his lips on every part of her body, to kiss him too. For a moment she swayed on her feet.

She gripped the desk even more tightly, her fingers biting into the hard wood. Grimly she said, 'No, you didn't, but then you've been very vague about my so-called "social duties". That won't be one of them.'

'Really?'

'As long as that's understood.'

In three long strides Sterling had covered the space between them. 'We've already established that sex was never a duty, Danielle.'

Her throat felt raw and her body burned. But she managed to say, 'Things have changed.'

He seized her shoulders. As he drew her towards him, she had no chance to escape—not that she wanted to.

His kisses were hard at first, bruising, as if an angry Sterling was punishing her for something she had done to him. But in seconds they changed to kisses that teased and tantalised, that drove fire through Danielle's body and chased all rational thought from her mind. Her arms lifted around his neck as she kissed him back with all the love and hunger that had been pent up inside her for too long.

She gasped when he released her—so abruptly that she nearly fell back against the desk. She gazed up at him, her tongue licking her lips, her eyes glazed with shock.

She was still trying to regain her composure when Sterling said harshly, 'For the record, sex will not be one of your duties. As to either of us wanting it—don't try telling me anything has changed in that respect. We'd both know you were lying.'

'You're a rotten swine, Sterling Tenassik!'

'If you say so.'

'I'm probably all sorts of a fool to go on this trip with you.'

'You can still back out.'

'I can't. I need the money and you know it. You have me over a barrel as far as that's concerned. It's the reason I've agreed to travel with you. The *only* reason.'

Sterling's eyes were oddly bleak, but Danielle did not notice it. 'I have to have your promise that you won't change your mind and cancel halfway through the trip,' he said.

A shiver went through her once more, but Danielle managed to hide it. 'You have my word,' she told him flatly.

'I need more than your word; I want your signature, Danielle.'

'What are you saying now?'

'I have a contract for you to sign.'

'Don't you trust me, Sterling?'

'You ran out on me once,' he reminded her pleasantly. Reaching for some papers at the side of the desk, he put them before her. 'There you are, Danielle.'

Incensed, she read the document over quickly, then looked up at Sterling. 'You must have been very sure of me if you had this drawn up ahead of time.'

'Hopeful.'

'You take some beating for arrogance,' Danielle said bitterly as she scrawled her signature at the bottom of the second page.

She was walking away from the desk when Sterling said, 'Why is the money so important to you, Danielle?'

For a moment the breath stopped in her throat. She was glad that her back was turned to him, so that he could not see her eyes.

'I want to know, Danielle.'

Only when she thought that she could meet his gaze did she turn her head. 'That shouldn't interest you, Sterling.'

His eyes were hooded, difficult to read. 'My interest is always aroused where you're concerned, Danielle. Why is the money so important?'

Danielle took a quick breath to control her sudden trembling. Then she said, 'All right, Sterling, I'll tell you why. I have a child.'

Beneath his tan Sterling was suddenly pale. For a moment he had the look of a man who had just taken a punch in the face.

'*My God!*' he exclaimed.

It was an effort to keep her voice on an even keel. 'We live with my parents but we need our own home. *That's* why I need money.'

'A child...' Sterling said roughly.

Danielle had not expected his reaction to be quite so intense. Unsteadily she said, 'The other evening I told you that someone was waiting for me.'

'I thought you meant a man.'

'I was talking about my little boy.'

Abruptly, Sterling pushed his chair away from the desk and stood up. His expression more severe than she had ever seen it, he stared down at Danielle.

After a long moment he asked aloofly, 'Why are you living with your parents? Why not with the father of your child?'

'That's none of your business,' Danielle said faintly.

Sterling's lips tightened. 'Tell me about this son of yours.'

If only he wouldn't tower above her so aggressively, Danielle thought. She shivered, then was still. 'His name is Toby,' she said in a low voice.

'Tell me more.'

'He has fair hair and blue eyes. I have a picture, if you'd like to see it...'

Sterling was silent as she handed him the photo she had deliberately brought to work with her, frowning as he looked down at the laughing child who bore so little resemblance to him.

'He looks like you,' he said at last.

'Yes.'

'How about his father?' His tone was icy now.

Danielle swallowed hard. 'There are ways in which they're similar.'

But those similarities—a quirking of the mouth when Toby laughed, a lifting of the eyebrows when he questioned something—were not obvious in a photo. It was unlikely that Sterling would recognise them even if he knew Toby well.

His expression was stony. 'How old is Toby?'

Danielle was so nervous now that she did not know if the words would make it past her lips. 'Three and a bit.'

Sterling took a quick step backwards. *'Three and a bit?'* he repeated disbelievingly.

'Yes.'

'When was he born?'

'Sterling . . .'

Suddenly he had closed the gap between them and was gripping her shoulders. *'When,* Danielle?'

So he had made the connection. Well, what had she expected? Sterling was no fool.

As she told him the date, she remembered that Toby had been born more than three weeks after the day he had been due. It was quite unusual, the doctor had told her at the time, to let an expectant mother go more than two weeks past her due date; but Toby had been particularly small, examination had suggested that he was not ready to be born, and after serious consideration the decision had been made to allow the baby to emerge when it was ready to.

'Nine months after we were together, Danielle?'

Had Sterling sounded eager, loving, excited at the thought that they might have produced a child together, she would not have hesitated to tell him the truth at that moment. As it was, his tone was so odd: flat, a little hard, as if he was contemptuous of what he was hearing. As if he was remembering the agreement they had made: no strings attached.

'Closer to ten months, actually,' she said unsteadily.

'I see,' he said grimly.

'You seem shocked.'

'That's putting it mildly. You were so sweet, so innocent, so trusting when we made love that last night. You actually had me believing you were a virgin. And I—' He stopped. When he continued, his expression was savage. 'All the time you had some other man on a string.'

'You don't understand—'

'Don't kid yourself, Danielle; I understand only too well. You slept with me, and back home some other man was waiting for you, keeping the bed warm until you returned.'

'No, I—'

'I understood you'd just got over some unhappy love affair, that you didn't want to get involved with someone new. But that wasn't it at all. You had a man in your life all the time. And you wanted the excitement of a holiday romance as well. No wonder you opted for our agreement; a second lover back home would have been difficult, to say the least. Unless, of course, you're used to juggling your men, in which case you might have managed.'

'Sterling—'

'Did you compare our prowess as lovers? Did you, Danielle? Did you tell him about me? Or did you play your little double game with Toby's father as well?'

His fingers bit into the soft skin of her upper arms. 'You say you don't live with Toby's father.'

'No.'

'Where is he, Danielle? Where is this man?'

And when she didn't answer he ground out, 'You're not married now; were you ever married to him?'

She shook her head.

An odd expression appeared in Sterling's eyes. It was gone in a second. 'What happens to Toby when we travel, Danielle?'

'*If* we travel my parents will look after him.'

'I see.'

She looked at him. 'I asked you a few minutes ago how long we'd be gone.'

'And I didn't give you an answer.'

'Now that I've told you about Toby, you can understand why I need to know,' she said urgently. 'It will be very difficult for me to be away from my child.'

'With your parents looking after him?'

'*He's my son*, Sterling. Little more than a baby. I can't just vanish from his life.'

Sterling's eyes glittered. 'If you're asking me to tie myself down to time, forget it.'

'But, Sterling—'

'You're being paid for your services,' he said crisply. 'Handsomely.'

Danielle pushed herself out of his hands. 'You really are a swine!' She flung the words at him as she ran to the door.

Irene and the others in the secretarial pool were agog with curiosity the next day when Danielle told them the reason why she was going to be absent from the office for a while. She would have liked to keep it from them, but there was no point in hiding something that would be common knowledge anyway the moment she and Sterling embarked on their travels.

'Lucky you!' Irene exclaimed. 'A holiday with the hunk!'

'It won't be a holiday,' Danielle defended herself abruptly. 'I'm only going as his secretary.'

'Lots of gorgeous clothes.'

'Which I probably won't have a chance to wear as I'll be so busy typing.'

'Will you get to keep them afterwards?' one of the other secretaries wanted to know.

'I hadn't thought about that. No, I shouldn't think so. I wouldn't want them anyway.'

It was a statement which the others all seemed to find most peculiar.

'You're so down on Mr Tenassik,' Irene giggled later, when they were alone together. 'I wonder if you aren't secretly falling in love with the guy...?'

'Don't say that!' The words emerged in a fierce rush.

Irene looked startled as she stared at Danielle's ashen face. But she said nothing more as she returned to her work.

Danielle began her shopping still haunted by the uneasy conviction that there was something odd about the trip that Sterling had planned—a thought that she tried to push from her mind as she walked into a boutique, the windows of which displayed clothes that she had only been able to admire until now because they were so expensive.

Danielle had always loved clothes. Possessed of a good eye for colour and style, window-shopping was one of her favourite pastimes. But, her financial situation being what it was, she had sewn most of her clothes herself until now, often from lovely fabrics which she managed to buy cheaply at sales. It was a new experience for her to try on expensive garments, aware that she could have anything she wanted.

Two days later she was ready to show Sterling her purchases. In the late afternoon, when she was certain that the rest of the staff would have left the office, she knocked on his door.

'I've been looking forward to this,' he said when he saw the shopping bags she was carrying.

'You might not be so pleased when you find out how much this little lot is going to be costing you.'

He laughed at that. 'I'll be pleased as long as the money was well spent. And I'll know that when you show me what you've bought. There's a room through there—' he gestured—'where you can change.'

Danielle stared at him in horror. 'You expect me to model the stuff?'

'Precisely.'

'No, Sterling! I refuse! Absolutely not!'

'Absolutely yes, Danielle.'

'This is silly. You're a man—what can you possibly know about a woman's clothes?'

'Enough to satisfy myself as to whether you'll look suitable for the occasion.'

'I don't like this,' Danielle said in a low voice.

Once more Sterling laughed, and this time she saw the gleam in his eyes. 'Start modelling,' he ordered.

In the end Danielle had no choice but to do as he asked. She modelled everything: trousers and blouses, a yellow blazer that teamed well with both trousers and a skirt, dresses for pool-side wear and for the evening. And, last of all, two swimsuits.

Sterling said very little as she appeared before him in one lovely outfit after another, but she saw the way his eyes went over her, particularly when she appeared in the swimsuits, and she wished she could stop the flush that rose in her cheeks.

'Well?' she asked, when she was dressed once more in the skirt and blouse she'd sewn herself.

'Very nice—most of it.'

'Meaning?'

'You have a great sense of style. You're naturally classy.'

'But? There *is* a "but" in there somewhere; I can hear it.'

'We are going to make a few changes.'

'*We?*' Danielle demanded. 'Are you saying you want me to take back these clothes?'

'Not exactly.' His eyes were warm with devilment. 'I'm going to help you get a few more.'

'No, Sterling! It isn't necessary. You've just told me I have a good sense of style. I have everything you asked me to buy. I don't need anything else.'

'I already told you, most of what you bought is very nice,' he agreed calmly.

'There's still that "but" in your voice.'

'Nice—without being zippy.'

'Zippy being a euphemism for sexy?'

'Quite.'

Danielle stared at him furiously. 'You do want some kind of call-girl after all. Money or not, I'm not the right person for you! Find someone else.'

In the end Sterling had his way. He would always have his way, Danielle reflected bitterly as she followed him into one of the most exclusive boutiques in the city. The prices here were known to be so high that she would never have ventured to cross the threshold.

They had already been to another store that morning, where Sterling had insisted that Danielle trade in the relatively modest swimsuits she had bought for bikinis so tiny that they left almost nothing to the imagination. She wondered what he had planned for her now.

It was Sterling who spotted the strapless black dress with the slit all the way up the thigh.

'Not for me,' Danielle muttered dismissively.

'I want to see you in it.'

She shook her head.

'Please, Danielle, try it on.' And the saleswoman, elegantly coiffed and clothed, sensing a possible sale, added her own words of persuasion.

By this time Danielle wanted nothing more than to leave the boutique, but it was clear that they would not do so until she had tried on the dress. Grimly, she marched into the fitting-room—all plush carpet, gilt-edged mirrors and muted colours—peeled off her clothes and slipped on the dress.

In front of the mirror, she gasped. She barely recognised herself. The dress moulded itself to her body as if it had been made for her, endowing her slender figure with a curvaceousness that she had never dreamed she possessed. In less than a minute Danielle, wholesome mother and competent secretary, had been transformed into Danielle, the sensuously seductive siren.

She stared at herself in wonder, knowing that she looked stunning. Without thinking about what she was doing, she smoothed her hands slowly down her body, seeing, as if for the first time, the soft swell of her breasts and the curve of her hips. Danielle was suddenly very excited. Without Sterling's urging, she would never have thought of trying on the dress. It was a shock to realise that she *liked* what she was seeing.

'Madam?' The saleswoman was at the door. 'The gentleman wondered if he could see you in the dress.'

'He cannot!'

Half a minute later the door opened. 'Did you tell him—?' Danielle started to say, stopping abruptly when she saw Sterling in the mirror. 'How dare you come in here?' she asked furiously.

'Since you wouldn't come out...' he answered her pleasantly. 'Let me look at you, Danielle.'

'No.' Instinctively, her hands lifted to cover breasts that were almost naked.

He took her hands, quite gently, and after a moment she let him drop them at her sides. 'Please,' he said, and took a few steps away from her.

She was restless as his eyes lingered on her body, travelling from her breasts to her waist and hips and then up her thighs in a gaze that was as intimate as if he were making love to her.

'That's enough,' she muttered abruptly.

'It is,' he agreed softly. 'I've seen as much as I need to.'

Aware that the saleswoman could be within earshot, Danielle hissed quietly, 'As long as you realise the dress isn't for me.'

Sterling's only answer was another intimate look before he retreated from the fitting-room.

It took Danielle longer than usual to get back into her own clothes, for her mind was in turmoil and her hands were trembling. As she brushed her hair back into place, she was almost contrarily relieved to see that the sexy siren had vanished. The image in the mirror was the familiar one—the one she felt comfortable with. And with her return to her own self the trembling stilled.

Anger flared within her when she emerged from the fitting-room to see Sterling slipping his credit card back into his wallet, but she waited until they were well out of the boutique before she confronted him. 'You bought the dress, didn't you?'

Sterling grinned at her. 'It will be delivered later today.'

'I won't accept delivery.'

'You won't have to; it's being sent to me.'

She looked up at him, her green eyes stormy . 'Why, Sterling? I told you it wasn't for me.'

'I disagree. Have you any idea how you look in that dress, Danielle? One glimpse of you and any normal man would go right out of his mind.'

'Including you?' The words were out before Danielle could stop them. She gazed at Sterling in horror, wondering how she could have been so *stupid* as to give voice to her thoughts.

His eyes gleamed with satisfaction. 'You'll have every opportunity to find out, I promise you.'

'No,' she said flatly, 'because I refuse to wear the dress.' Her voice was a little unsteady now. 'And don't make anything of that question I just asked.'

'No?' he drawled.

'I didn't mean it.'

'Sure of that, Danielle?'

'Completely.'

'Perhaps I'd enjoy being driven out of my mind.'

'Find someone else to do it.' Her eyes were still stormy. 'As for the dress, it's too bad you paid all that money; I hope you manage to get a refund.'

'I don't need one. I won't be returning it.'

'I made it clear I didn't want it. I won't wear it.'

'I want you to take it on our trip.'

'Absolutely not! I mean it. Do you know how I felt in the boutique, Sterling? Cheap. Degraded and embarrassed. I knew exactly what the saleswoman was thinking, and I was ashamed.'

'Don't overreact, Danielle.'

'I'm not saying half of what I feel. Not a fraction. I resent what you're doing to me, Sterling. If I didn't need your money, I'd back out of the agreement this very minute.'

'You'll go through with it all the same.'

'Only because I have to. But I won't sell my soul for your money.'

'Meaning?'

'The skimpy bikinis are one thing, though I wouldn't have chosen them myself. But if you think I'll pack the black dress you're mistaken. I refuse to have it in my suitcase.'

CHAPTER FOUR

DANIELLE was startled when she heard the doorbell ring.

'You're twenty minutes early,' she accused as she opened the door for Sterling.

'The traffic was easy for once.' An eyebrow lifted quizzically. 'You seem bothered.'

'It's just that I'm not quite ready. It's been one of those mornings—everything going wrong. I was hoping you'd be late. That way—'

Danielle broke off as her parents appeared, first her mother, then her father. A little too quickly, she made the introductions. 'Sterling—my parents, Anne and Barry Payne. Mom and Dad, this is Sterling Tenassik.'

Her parents were looking at Sterling, their expressions wary, and then her father said, 'Mr Tenassik . . .'

'Sterling, please . . .' he said with an easy smile, and put out his hand.

A second later a little boy ran into the room.

A moment passed. Then Sterling said, 'And you must be Toby.'

All at once there was tension in the air. Glancing at Sterling, Danielle flinched at the hardness in his eyes, the rigidity in his jaw.

If only he had agreed to meet her outside the office building, as she had suggested. But he had been surprisingly stubborn: she would have her suitcase, and he intended to pick her up at her home. She would take a cab, she'd said, a hint of panic in her voice, but Sterling had refused to hear of it. She wondered now whether his purpose in coming to the house had been to meet her child. *Their* child.

The fair-haired, blue-eyed little boy looked up at the dark-haired, dark-eyed man. 'Want to see my fire-truck? Mommy gave it to me.'

For a long moment the tall man looked down at Toby. Danielle held her breath as she waited for him to reject his son.

Without warning the little boy took the man's hand. 'Come see the fire-truck?'

Transfixed, Danielle stared at the tiny hand in the big one. This had to be a dream, she thought wildly.

Suddenly, as if the child's innocence touched him in some way, Sterling's hardness vanished and he grinned. 'Sure. I like fire-trucks.'

'I can't make it run,' Toby said as Danielle let out her breath.

'I'll take a look at it later,' his grandfather said quickly.

'Why don't I take a look?' Sterling said. And with a glance at Danielle he added, 'You did say you weren't quite ready?'

'Not quite.' Her voice shook.

'There's a nice smooth path in the garden; I saw it as I came in. Mind if we take the fire-truck out there?'

Danielle watched disbelievingly as Toby and Sterling went outside. Seconds later, on trembling legs, she went to her room. There were a few last-minute things that still needed packing, but she didn't attend to them right away.

Her room had a view over the garden. Still finding it hard to believe what she was seeing, she watched as Toby showed his father the toy that she had given him earlier that morning.

Evidently Sterling knew something about the workings of mechanical toys, for in less than a minute he had the fire-truck launched on its way. It was painted a particularly vivid shade of red, and its bell gave off a series of piercing shrieks as it went.

And then Sterling was squatting beside Toby, and they were laughing together as they watched the fire-truck career along the garden path.

Watching them together, father and son, Danielle felt a small squeeze of pain in her chest. No stranger seeing them now would have been able to guess how angry and contemptuous this relaxed and playful Sterling had been on learning about her child.

'Quite a scene.'

Danielle turned as her mother came up beside her. 'Quite a scene,' she agreed drily.

'I like him, Danielle.'

'Mom...'

'I didn't think I would, but I do.'

'He knows how to turn on the charm,' Danielle said bitterly.

'It's a lot more than that, sweetheart. He doesn't have to play with Toby.'

'I know that...' she conceded grudgingly.

'Will you tell him, Danielle?'

'No.' The answer came without hesitation. 'There was a moment a few days ago when I thought that I might. And then I realised it was no use. You didn't hear the things he said to me, Mom. Just as you weren't with us when we talked in Hawaii. Sterling is getting on surprisingly well with Toby, I admit, but he'd be appalled if he knew that Toby was his own child.'

Toby was a little upset when his mother said goodbye to him, but he had his new fire-truck to console him, and his grandparents had promised to take him out for an ice cream. It was Danielle who had to blink back tears as she hugged her small son.

'I'll be back just as soon as possible,' she assured him.

She said goodbye to her parents, then went out to the street, where Sterling was putting her suitcase, still smelling of new leather, in the boot of his sporty red car. Minutes later they were driving away from the house.

'Nice child,' he commented as they drove southwards, away from San Francisco.

'He's a darling,' she agreed, and then said, 'You surprised me, Sterling.'

'Because I played with your son?'

'You were so *pleasant*. But then, I suppose you were putting on a very good act.'

The eyes that turned momentarily to hers were hard. 'Not an act, Danielle. Toby is easy to like.'

Hope flared inside her. 'What are you saying?' she asked unsteadily.

'It's not his fault that his mother was playing fast and loose.'

Danielle chose not to answer him. Her cheeks hot with anger, she turned her face to the window. With Sterling's last words, gone was any lingering idea of telling him the truth about his child.

It was a long while before they spoke again.

Stopping the car beside a pair of handsome stone gates, Sterling turned to Danielle. 'Time to talk.'

She turned listless eyes to him. 'Haven't we done enough of that already?'

His lips tightened. 'This is something else. Regarding the place we're going to.'

She made a small gesture. 'Is this it?'

'A wine estate, as you can see. The owner, Marcus Renfield, has vast interests apart from vineyards; for one thing, he's a powerful man in the hotel industry.'

'And you're expecting him to give us his advertising and bring prosperity to our own company.'

'With some tough bargaining and good presentation on my part,' Sterling said drily.

'I'm sure you'll succeed. Don't you always get what you want, Sterling?'

'Not always.' His gaze rested on her face in a look that was infinitely disturbing. 'Which doesn't mean I give up trying.' Another disturbing look. 'But it's time you knew your function here.'

'You've told me that already. I'll be secretary to the man who's going to do the presentation. Isn't that it, Sterling?'

'Not quite.'

There was something odd in Sterling's voice. Danielle tried to make out his expression, but his eyes were shuttered now and impossible to read. Without knowing quite why, she felt herself tense.

'Actually, your secretarial role will be a very minor one,' he said at length.

'I don't understand.'

'Virtually non-existent in fact. If you do any typing, and you probably won't, Marcus and his wife won't know anything about it.'

Danielle sat up straight. 'What on earth are you talking about? Why am I here if not to do your work?'

His gaze was on her face once more. 'Your main purpose is social.'

'You did say I'd have some social duties,' Danielle remembered, 'which I'd learn about in due course. What exactly are you expecting me to do?'

'Pose as my fiancée,' Sterling said crisply.

Danielle jerked quite violently in her seat. *'What?'* she asked disbelievingly.

'You heard me.'

'You can't possibly expect me to play the part of your fiancée!'

'It's exactly what I do expect.'

'No, Sterling, absolutely not!'

'It's why you're here, Danielle.'

'I won't do it!'

'Is the thought of being engaged to me so repulsive?' Sterling's expression was aloof now and a little forbidding.

Danielle's throat had dried and tears pricked her eyes. She had dreamed so often that Sterling would come back into her life, but her wildest fantasies had never conjured up a scenario as cruel as this one.

She waited till she was quite certain that she had herself under control before answering. 'Repulsive? The question doesn't deserve an answer. I...I think you'd better take me right back to San Francisco.'

'Several hours of driving?' he asked mockingly. His face was bleak—not that she made anything of it.

'However long it takes. Mr Renfield hasn't seen us; he doesn't know we're here. We could easily turn back.'

'He knows we're on our way; so does his wife.'

'In that case, go and make your excuses. Say whatever you wish, Sterling. Pretend I'm ill if you like, but take me back to San Francisco.'

'No, Danielle.'

'You can't possibly expect me to go through with this.'

'I do. What's more, I expect you to perform convincingly and to the best of your ability.'

'I won't! I refuse!'

'We have an agreement, Danielle—one that you put your name to in writing. There are things you seem to have forgotten—' he gave her a hard look '—but you can't have forgotten that.'

'No...'

'It's settled, then.'

'It's far from settled.' She was outraged. 'It's not settled at all. You tricked me into this, Sterling.'

'I offered you money—a very substantial amount of money—which you accepted.'

'I didn't have much choice,' she said bitterly.

'People always have choices. You must have wondered why I was offering you so much more than your regular salary, and yet you accepted all the same.'

'I did ask.'

'You gave in without much of a fight.'

'If I'd known the truth—' She stopped.

'Would you have turned me down?'

'Yes.' Her voice shook.

His face was bleaker still. 'I don't think so, Danielle. You were very angry when I taunted you about having a price tag, and I said I wouldn't do it again, but the fact remains that once the price was high enough you agreed to my offer. With surprisingly few questions asked, I might add. So now it's my turn for questions. Why weren't you more curious? Why didn't you insist on knowing the exact nature of your duties? Why didn't you insist on answers? Of course we both know the reason—my offer was very attractive.'

Even with the air-conditioning on it was very hot in the car, yet Danielle knew that the flush in her cheeks stemmed solely from anger and embarrassment. Glaring furiously at Sterling, she wondered how it was possible to love a man so deeply without understanding him at all.

'It seems I'm trapped,' she said wildly.

'If that's the way you choose to look at it.'

'Is there another way?'

'This happens to be one of the most beautiful wine estates in California, and the Renfields are very pleasant hosts. You could decide to enjoy yourself.'

'How can I enjoy it,' she demanded, 'when I hate what you're asking me to do? Why is it necessary, anyway?'

Sterling pushed a hand through his hair. 'I haven't told you much about the Renfields; it's time I did. Marcus is very much older than his wife. She and I . . . were once good friends.'

'Judging by your tone, you were more than friends.' Deliberate briskness concealed a pain that stabbed at Danielle's heart.

'Good friends,' Sterling repeated firmly. 'The fact is, Lisa Renfield is not what you might call a faithful wife.'

'She was married and your mistress.'

'I said she was a friend.'

'I think I understand the relationship.' She paused, then tried to ask casually, 'Is . . . is she beautiful?'

'Very beautiful indeed.' Sterling grinned.

Danielle swallowed hard. 'I think I see.'

'Do you?'

'Not that difficult, is it? This advertising deal means a lot to you, and you won't let anything get in the way of it. If Marcus Renfield were to guess that you'd had an affair with his wife, he'd boot you out before you could do any business. What better camouflage than a brand-new and adoring fiancée?'

'Your powers of deduction amaze me,' Sterling mocked.

'Not much deduction needed. Does Marcus know about the engagement?'

'Not yet.'

'Lisa does, of course.'

'She doesn't know either.'

'Good grief! You mean you didn't warn her? Why not, Sterling?'

'It didn't seem necessary.'

Danielle put her head in her hands. When she looked up again she was pale. 'How could you do this to me, Sterling? Don't my feelings matter to you at all?'

'A strange question coming from you, of all people, Danielle. Where was your concern for my feelings when you walked out on me?'

Evidently his pride had been more badly hurt than she had ever anticipated. Sterling had wanted a proper goodbye before Danielle left his bed and walked out of his life for ever.

'We've been over that,' she said tightly. 'I did what seemed right to me at the time.'

'And this seems right to me now.'

'It won't work, Sterling.'

'It will have to,' he said, so firmly that she understood that there was no point in continuing the argument.

'I hope you're not expecting me to act all lovey-dovey, the starry-eyed fiancée of the great Sterling Tenassik. My God, Sterling, why didn't you go out and hire an actress? A professional worth her salt would play the part a lot better than I ever could.'

His jawline was hard and inflexible. 'You acted very well four years ago, Danielle. I almost believed that you—'

'That I what?' She was breathless suddenly.

'It doesn't matter. Not now. Just play your role the way you did then and you'll have our hosts convinced. Oh, there's one more thing.' Putting his hand in his pocket, he drew out a small velvet box which he gave to her.

Danielle gasped when she saw what was in the box: a diamond ring, the diamond beautifully set and surrounded by tiny emeralds. It was without a doubt the most beautiful ring she had ever seen. The diamond was also the biggest.

'You didn't have to give me this.' Her voice shook.

'Put it on, Danielle,' he said, very softly.

'Sterling . . .'

She looked up at him, her eyes shimmering. In that moment the only reality was the unexpected tenderness of the man beside her on the seat, and the fact that she loved him so much that she sometimes thought her heart would break with loving him.

'Put it on,' he said again. And when she hesitated he added, 'The Renfields are waiting for us.'

Sanity returned, and with it the full realisation of the charade upon which she was embarking.

She tried to thrust the ring back at him. 'I don't want it!'

'I want you to wear it.'

'Because Marcus and Lisa have to believe in us? Won't they see the ring and realise the diamond is just glass?'

'Glass, Danielle?'

'It has to be glass, hasn't it? Or at least some kind of fake. You'd hardly have gone out and bought a real diamond for a brief, sham engagement.'

'Would it matter if it were fake?' His dark eyes were intent.

'Heavens, no! If I were in love with a man, the last thing I'd care about would be an engagement ring. I wouldn't care if he didn't give me a ring at all. My only concern would be the commitment we were making.' Eyes bright with challenge, she lifted her chin at him. 'In our case there is no commitment.'

Sterling was silent for so long that Danielle began to wonder if he had nothing more to say. She saw the way his gaze swept her face, lingering too long on her lips, moving downwards over her throat. Restlessly, she looked away from him.

'Put on the ring,' he said at last.

'I can't . . .'

Ignoring the protest, he leaned towards her, reached for her left hand and placed the lovely ring on her third finger.

'There now, we're engaged.'

'No, Sterling, this can never . . .'

The rest of the sentence was stifled as he pulled her towards him. She closed her eyes as he began to kiss her—long, slow, exploratory kisses, so intoxicating that a hot tide of desire flared instantly to life inside her. Danielle did not even try to resist the tongue that probed her lips, persuading them to part; she parted them willingly. As one kiss merged into another, she arched towards Sterling, kissing him too, oblivious to everything except desire and sensation and a desperate hunger.

When he drew back she felt bereft. Without thinking, she leaned towards him. Sterling gave a little hiss, and Danielle's eyes snapped open. She saw his face, pale and tight, and when she pressed the back of her left hand over her lips the huge stone was cold and hard against her hot skin.

'My God!' Danielle whispered, appalled at the realisation that she had, for the duration of Sterling's kisses, lost all touch with reality.

'Well . . .' Sterling said.

Danielle jerked away from him. Stiffly, she sat as close to the passenger door as she could. 'Is that all you have to say?' she demanded furiously.

'What would you like me to say, Danielle?'

'*Nothing!* No, that's not true; I have to know—why did you do it?'

'Kiss you? Isn't it usual to seal an engagement with a kiss?'

'Not a sham engagement. And not that kind of kiss.' Her voice shook.

'Why the sudden protest? You gave every bit as good as you got.'

'I—' She stopped; there was nothing she could say.

'The Renfields will be impressed if you kiss me like that.'

'I won't be kissing you. I don't even know how I... You had no damn right, Sterling.'

'Who's talking of rights, Danielle? Either you wanted it as much as I did or else you're the actress you say I should have hired in your stead. A damn good actress, by the way. Go on acting just like that, Danielle, and you'll have our hosts fooled.' He paused, then said drily, 'You might even fool me as well.'

Sterling turned the key in the ignition once more. As he drove through the stone gates and began to negotiate the long, winding drive, Danielle took her cosmetic purse from her handbag. When she had combed her hair and put on fresh lipstick, she turned her head sideways and pretended to be interested in the view beyond her window.

Tall trees lined the drive. Beyond them, on either side, well-tended vineyards stretched all the way to the horizon, bearing the promise of fine wines. If Danielle had not been quite so agitated, she would have understood why Sterling had called the estate one of the most beautiful in California.

As it was, she was just relieved that she had regained some measure of composure by the time they drew up a little way from the main house. It was a beautiful house; even in her distress Danielle was able to see that. Spanish-style—white walls, courtyards and wrought-iron gates—it blended perfectly with the surrounding countryside.

The door of the house opened and a man walked out— a tall man with a shock of greying hair and deeply tanned skin. A handsome man, who wore his aura of great wealth as easily as he wore his casually elegant clothes.

'Marcus,' Sterling said in an undertone. 'All set, Danielle?'

She threw him a provocative smile. 'Poised in the wings, ready to make my entrance on stage the moment I'm given the cue.'

Sterling's eyes glittered ominously, the sight giving Danielle a moment of immeasurable satisfaction.

'See that you behave yourself,' he growled. And then he had opened his door and was going towards the other man, putting out his hand and saying, 'Hello, Marcus.'

'Sterling. Good to see you. Let's get your luggage out of the car, then we can go up to the house.'

'There's just one thing.' Sterling gestured. 'I've brought a guest; I didn't think you'd mind.'

Marcus turned his head in the direction of the car. 'A guest?'

Sterling opened Danielle's door, and she got out and extended her hand and said a little awkwardly, 'I'm Danielle Payne. And you didn't say... I hope you really don't mind my being here, Mr Renfield?'

The older man was looking at her curiously, his speculative eyes making no attempt to hide his approval. 'Of course I don't mind. We have a big house, and we do a lot of entertaining—Sterling knows an extra guest is no trouble. Besides, a very beautiful young woman is always a pleasure. Call me Marcus, please. Danielle, did you say?'

He was still holding her hand. Feeling more than a little uncomfortable now, Danielle moved away from him as unobtrusively as she could.

And then Sterling was putting his arm around her shoulders, drawing her easily against him, intimately, as if physical contact was an integral part of their relationship. Danielle's stiffening was instinctive, but as warning fingers dug into her shoulder, reminding her of her role, she tried to relax.

'Danielle and I are engaged,' Sterling said.

'Well!' The speculation in the other man's eyes increased. 'I had no idea; I don't believe Lisa knows either. You're a crafty one, Sterling, springing a surprise like this on us. Lisa *will* be surprised.'

The unknown Lisa. Sterling's once-upon-a-time very good friend. Judging by Marcus's reaction, Lisa would be very surprised indeed. To her husband's evident satisfaction.

'Now we really must get your luggage out of the car,' Marcus was saying. 'And then we'll have something to drink. Danielle, my dear, you must be parched. I believe that Lisa has—' He turned his head. 'Why, here she is now.'

A woman had emerged from the house. 'Is that Sterling?' she was calling in a husky voice.

They were facing in a different direction now, and the sun shone in Danielle's eyes, so that her vision of the other woman was blurred. She had no more than an impression of a tall figure with dark hair.

'Hi, Lisa,' Sterling called back, his greeting casual and friendly.

'Sterling brought along a surprise,' Lisa's husband said.

And then they were all three walking towards the house. Sterling's arm was still firmly around Danielle's shoulders as Marcus said, 'My wife—Lisa. And this is Danielle Payne, honey—Sterling's fiancée.'

Danielle caught an edge of malicious amusement in Marcus's tone, but she had no time to think about it at that moment.

'Fiancée!' Lisa sounded shocked.

But she could not have been any more shocked than Danielle herself as she recognised the woman who had been with Sterling on his first day in the office.

She tried to take a step backwards but Sterling's arm stopped her. Involuntarily, she looked up at him. He was ready for her, the dark eyes enigmatic as they caught hers. They contained a warning: Say the wrong thing and you'll regret it.

Lisa was the first to recover from the shock. For one long moment she stared at Danielle with an expression that was undisguisedly hostile. Then she was smiling— a brilliant smile, even if it did not make it past her lips.

Clapping her hands, she trilled, 'How lovely! Congratulations, Danielle. Sterling, you old dog, so you're finally going to the altar! Danielle, you won't mind if I kiss the groom?'

Without waiting for permission from either Danielle or Sterling, or from her husband, for that matter, she closed the space between them. Elbowing Danielle out of the way, she put her arm around Sterling's neck and kissed him long and thoroughly on the lips.

When she let him go and took a step away—not very far away, Danielle noticed—Sterling shot Danielle a mischievous grin. It was evident that he had had no objection at all to the kiss; if anything, he had enjoyed it. And if Marcus objected there was nothing in his manner to suggest it. Danielle was the only one who was at all disturbed by the intimacy of what had happened, she realised. She felt a little ill.

'The luggage is still in the car,' Marcus told his wife. 'We were about to get it.'

'I'll send someone out to do it,' Lisa said. 'Just as well I put you in one of the bigger guest-rooms, Sterling. It has a nice double bed, Danielle. Not too big, though—

just the right size for an engaged couple who like to be snug.'

Danielle found her voice. 'I would like a separate room.'

Marcus and Lisa stared at her in amazement. Danielle did not trust herself to look at Sterling.

'Good grief!' Marcus exclaimed. 'Aren't you two living together? I thought it was the done thing for people to share a bed these days, married or not. And sometimes when they're married to other people. Not so, Lisa, my pet?'

But Danielle didn't want to hear Lisa's reply. Only a few minutes in the company of the Renfields and already she was feeling thoroughly out of her depth among people who were clearly very much more sophisticated than she would ever be.

Still without looking at Sterling, she said, 'I guess I'm an old-fashioned girl.'

Lisa laughed—a husky laugh that was as sexy as her speaking voice. 'An old-fashioned girl! How very funny.'

'I think it's delightful,' her husband said, that malice back in his tone.

'Sterling Tenassik, of all people.' Lisa laughed again. 'How ever did you catch him, Danielle? Not in bed, obviously. You must let me in on your secret; I'm dying to know. When the men are busy talking business you and I can have lots of nice little woman-to-woman chats.'

Danielle, who could not begin to imagine herself having a woman-to-woman chat with Lisa Renfield—it was hard to imagine that Lisa would have any woman-friends at all—was relieved when Marcus said, 'Lisa can show Danielle to her room while I tell you where to park the car, Sterling; you'll want to get it out of the sun.'

Danielle was standing at the window of her room, looking out over a very beautiful garden, when someone knocked. Before she could call out, Sterling walked in, carrying her suitcase.

'How could you?' she threw at him, the moment he had closed the door behind him.

'How could I what, Danielle?'

'As if you don't know! How could you bring me here?'

'We've been over this; you know why I brought you.'

'That woman... Lisa...'

'What about her?'

'She was in the office with you that first day. She's the woman you were kissing.'

'Actually,' Sterling observed quietly, 'we hadn't kissed when you walked in on us. Besides, she was about to do the kissing.'

'Do you really think I care who was kissing whom?' Danielle responded impatiently. 'That's just a minor detail.'

'Sometimes minor details matter.'

'Not this one. The point is, why didn't you tell me who she was?'

'I did.' There was an enigmatic expression in the dark eyes that studied her. 'I told you her name was Lisa. I said she was a good friend.'

'Good friend as in mistress; we've been over that too.'

'You're making assumptions, Danielle.' His voice was smooth and infinitely dangerous.

'The right ones,' she said tersely. 'I may not be as wordly-wise as you and your friends, but there are things I know. Why didn't you tell me, Sterling?'

'I did tell you,' he said again. 'You knew there was going to be a woman; you just didn't realise you'd recognise her. But since that's not exactly earth-shattering, what's bothering you?'

She looked at him, wishing she didn't love him so desperately, wishing she had never got herself into this mess.

'You did tell me,' she acknowledged at last. 'The thing is...I understood Lisa to be a—a *friend*, if that's the word you insist on using, from the past. You were *once* good friends; that's the way you put it to me. It never occurred to me that you were still seeing her.'

'I haven't said I am.'

'I don't want to get into word games, Sterling. You know exactly what I mean. Lisa was in your office recently, and the two of you were kissing—or about to.'

'I'm not sure I understand why you're so upset, Danielle. Why should it matter that Lisa is the woman you saw me with, and that the friendship isn't all that long in the past?'

Danielle shifted her gaze in order to conceal the pain that racked her, knifing at her chest and her throat. The thought of Sterling with any woman other than herself was unbearable, whether the affair was recent or not. The fact was that this particular woman had a face, and since the day she had walked unannounced into Sterling's office Danielle had been unable to put that face out of her mind.

'You're not jealous by any chance?' Sterling drawled.

'*Jealous?*' Danielle hissed. 'Of you? Of Lisa? Why on earth would I be jealous?'

'That's the question I ask myself.' He was watching her intently. 'Why would you mind if there is a woman in my life? *If* there is a woman, and I haven't said that there is.'

'You don't have to. And I *don't* mind; I couldn't care less. It's just...'

'Just what, Danielle?' Sterling prompted.

'I hate the deceit. The subterfuge. I loathe playing games. Is it really necessary, Sterling?'

'It is,' he told her flatly. 'And if your conscience is bothering you remind yourself of the money you're being paid and I'm sure you'll act your part to perfection.'

'Talking of which—' Danielle pulled the beautiful ring from her finger '—I won't be wearing this when I'm not acting.'

His jaw tightened. 'Would it be such a hardship to wear the diamond I gave you?'

'You mean the fake. Say it as it is, Sterling; we both know what it is. And yes, it would be a hardship because the whole thing is such a farce. At least when I'm alone I won't have to be reminded of the sham every time I look at my hand.'

Going to the bedside table, she shoved the ring in a drawer. When she looked at Sterling once more, she saw that his expression was grim.

'I won't lose it, if that's what you're thinking,' she told him. 'I'll take care of it while it's in my possession—which I hope won't be very long.'

'As long as it takes,' he said.

The oddness of his tone made her uncertain. 'You mean until Marcus agrees to your advertising proposals?'

Unexpectedly Sterling grinned. 'As I said, as long as it takes.'

'How long do you think that will be, Sterling?'

His eyes held hers in a gaze that was disturbingly penetrating, all the more so because she did not understand what it meant. 'It depends,' was all he said.

He was walking to the door when he turned back to her. 'Still talking of parts,' he said, 'you couldn't wait, could you, to tell our hosts that you had to have a separate room?'

'I thought it best to make things quite clear.'

'We're supposed to be engaged.'

'My part doesn't extend to sharing a room.'

'That's such a terrible thought, is it? As terrible as our engagement and having to wear my ring?'

Deep inside Danielle a great trembling began. Also an intense and frightening hunger. She had to draw upon all her resources to present an outward composure.

'Yes.' Her tone was low.

In an instant Sterling was right in front of her. His hands went to her shoulders, drawing her against him, so close that she could feel the hard length of his body, warm and pulsing, against her own. Involuntarily, she closed her eyes. She felt so dizzy that if he had not been holding her she would have swayed.

'It wasn't always a terrible thought,' Sterling grated. 'I remember when you came to my room of your own free will. When you were as eager to make love as I was.'

'Don't...' she whispered.

'I believe you'd come to my room again if I asked you.'

'You're wrong,' she protested jerkily.

'Am I, Danielle? Or are you being dishonest with yourself?'

Without waiting for an answer, he thrust her abruptly from him. Seconds later he had left the room.

CHAPTER FIVE

In Hawaii Danielle had quickly discovered that it would take more than a little resolve to keep herself emotionally detached from Sterling.

When he joined her on the beach the morning after their dinner in the restaurant, she realised that he was every bit as attractive as she'd remembered. Not handsome—at least not in the conventional sense of the word—he was nonetheless hard and tough and tremendously sexy, virile in a way which struck at some deep, hitherto unsuspected core inside Danielle.

And then she saw the way he was looking at her, his sparkling eyes caressing her body in a manner that was intensely male and approving, and she realised, with a little jolt of pleasure, that the attraction was far from being one-sided. Which did not alter the fact that they had a first-name-only relationship and that they had both agreed that things would never progress further than that.

He reached down to her, and she put her hands in his and let him pull her to her feet. For a few seconds they stood very close together, not quite touching, yet so close that they were acutely aware of each other's sun-warmed body. Seconds later, as if the atmosphere was a little too charged, they drew apart.

Hand in hand, they walked along the beach, laughing at the patterns their feet made in the firm sand near the water, at a few gulls squabbling furiously over a fish, and at a wave that rushed in further than the rest and drenched their bare legs with foam. There was so much to laugh about. Sterling had the gift of telling a joke well, and Danielle had a fund of anecdotes which he seemed to find amusing.

They swam, laughing again as the waves buffeted her smaller body against his larger one, but beneath the laughter Danielle was conscious of her heart hammering in her chest.

They came out of the sea and found a sun-warmed rock where they sat and let their bodies dry. A vendor walked by and Sterling bought two ice creams.

When Danielle had finished eating, Sterling looked at her and said, 'Hey, you have a white moustache—did you know?' And before she could stop him he had bent his head and was licking the remnants of her ice cream from the skin above her lips.

And then his tongue touched her once more, slowly and unbearably sensuously this time, exploring the shape of her lips. In seconds Danielle's blood had turned to fire and she felt an unfamiliar tightening in her groin. Sterling lifted his head and she looked at him wordlessly, and their eyes held for a long moment. Then he was pulling her to her feet and saying, 'Time for another swim.'

By the third day of the holiday, Danielle no longer attempted to deny to herself the excitement she experienced every time she was close to Sterling, or the erotic dreams that came to her in the night, or the way her blood raced whenever he kissed her. Once she saw a man who reminded her of John, and she was astonished to realise that she had not given John a serious thought since meeting Sterling. It was obvious that whatever she had once felt for her erstwhile fiancé she had not loved him. Certainly, she had never felt the longings that she was experiencing now.

One day followed another, each lovelier and more exciting than the one that preceded it. Every day they did something different: they explored lush landscapes and hiked up an ancient crater; they went horse-riding, and spent a lovely evening sampling delicious Polynesian foods; Sterling taught Danielle to snorkel, and they spent many hours in the water, marvelling at exotic fish.

The last day of the holiday was approaching and they decided to make it special: dinner at the restaurant where they had had their first meal together, then dancing, and afterwards a midnight swim.

They came out of the water that final night with their arms around each other. It was a beautiful night, the air sweet, the sky full of stars. As usual, they were laughing. They looked at each other in the dark and at the same moment the laughter died in their throats. Their arms tightened their hold and they stood together, two wet, throbbing bodies, communicating the same unspoken urgency of need and desire.

'Come to my room, Danielle.' Sterling's voice was hoarse.

They had long since gone beyond the stage of the friendly goodnight kiss; every day had seen their embraces become more passionate, but until now they had always understood that there had to be certain limits to their lovemaking. Tonight, Danielle knew, there could be no restraint.

In utter silence for once they went to Sterling's hotel. Once there, they hurried to his room. The moment the door was closed they began to kiss and explore with all the frenzy of lovers who knew there was a time limit to their lovemaking.

A virgin though she was, Danielle made no attempt to hold back when Sterling peeled off her swimsuit, laid her on his bed and gathered her naked body to his. The moment of fulfilment surpassed her wildest dreams, sweeping her with ecstasy and a joy like nothing she had ever imagined.

Afterwards they lay in each other's arms, caressing each other until they made love again. And after that they slept.

Danielle was the first to wake. When she opened her eyes the light of early dawn was filtering through the curtains. For a moment she did not know where she was. And then she became aware that the heaviness across her chest was Sterling's arm, the warm body surrounding hers was Sterling's, the bed in which she lay was Sterling's bed.

For a long time she lay quite still, listening to his breathing, inhaling the scent of him through her nostrils, delighting in the virile feel of him. She smiled to herself as she recalled the memories of the night they had shared. She could not remember an occasion when she had felt so utterly feminine, so vitally alive, so wonderfully fulfilled. Only Sterling, her love, her love for ever, could make her feel this way.

Her love... The smile vanished in a second as reality struck. Appalled, Danielle turned her head to look at the sleeping man, his tousled hair merging with hers on the pillow, his arm flung across her breasts. The terms they had discussed the first evening were branded in words of fire on her mind. First names only. No exchange of addresses. No strings of any kind. Terms mutually and willingly agreed to. Not once in all the time since then had Sterling given any indication that he regretted them.

And now the holiday was ending. Today was the day of farewell. Could she manage the parting with a smile and a jest and a few lightly spoken words? Great holiday, nice meeting you, hope we meet again some time?

Tense now, Danielle listened to the steady sound of Sterling's breathing and knew that there was no way she could say goodbye to him without breaking down. He murmured something in his sleep. Danielle touched his arm, willing the feel of his skin to remain in her memory for the rest of her life.

Then gently, very gently, she moved out from under his arm. Silently, so as not to wake him, she slipped on her clothes. On bare feet she tiptoed to the door. One hand was on the doorhandle when she turned, then went back to the bed and kissed him. She had to force herself to leave the room after that.

She cried all the way back to her hotel. The concierge looked up curiously as she passed the desk, but she did not stop. It did not take her long to pack.

When she checked out of the hotel, she made it clear that under no circumstances whatsoever were her name and address to be divulged to anyone. There was the very remote possibility that despite their agreement Sterling might, after all, want to retain some kind of contact. She could not bear the thought of him popping in and out of her life on a casual basis, treating her as just one of his many female friends.

A month after her precipitate departure from the island, Danielle learned that she was expecting a child. Dazed, she emerged from the doctor's office and went to a nearby park where she sat with her hands folded over her as yet non-existent belly.

Only then, when it was too late, did she remember that Sterling had murmured something about having no protection; she had said it didn't matter, from which he must have deduced—incorrectly—that she was already protected.

One magical night of lovemaking, and now a baby was growing inside her. Later, when the shock had worn off and she could think more clearly, she would worry about practicalities. In the park, with her hands on her stomach, there was only one thought in her mind: the man she had fallen so desperately in love with was not completely lost to her after all; her child would be a permanent reminder of its father.

A knock on the door jolted Danielle from her memories. 'Marcus and Lisa are waiting for us on the patio,' Sterling called.

It was time to psych herself up for an afternoon with her once-upon-a-time lover and their glamorous hosts. She could only hope that she was up to playing her part.

Briefly, she wondered what to wear, before deciding on one of her new sundresses—a pretty yellow and white striped garment which she teamed with a pair of big yellow earrings.

She was almost at the patio when she remembered the ring. Her expression grim, she returned to her room, retrieved the ring from the drawer and shoved it on her finger. A ray of afternoon sun slanted through the window, striking the ring and making it sparkle. Danielle looked at it in astonishment: it had never occurred to her that a fake diamond could shine so brilliantly. She left the room once more, shutting the door a little too hard, and made her way through the house to the patio.

She stopped in the archway that led onto a wide, glass-enclosed area bright with colourful shrubs in tall clay tubs. She stood so still that they did not see her at first, Sterling, Marcus and Lisa sitting in deep white wicker chairs, close together and deep in discussion.

Sterling must have made a joke because the other two laughed, and Lisa put her hand on Sterling's bare arm. Even after the laughter ended the long, manicured fingernails remained where they were. Curiously, Marcus did not seem to object to the intimacy, and Sterling did nothing to end it.

It was only when Danielle took a step forward that the others looked up, their conversation halting in mid-sentence.

'We were beginning to wonder what had happened to you,' Lisa said, her eyes glistening with a kind of venomous amusement. Her hand, Danielle noted, remained on Sterling's arm.

It was left to Sterling to remove it. Rising from his chair, he came towards Danielle. 'Darling,' he said.

She stiffened at the phony endearment.

'Relax,' Sterling, with his back to Marcus and Lisa, warned in an undertone. 'You're supposed to be happy to see me.'

A little too late, Danielle remembered the part she was being paid to play. With an effort she loosened fists that had clenched without her knowing it, smiled up at

Sterling, and wondered if her hosts really took her to be happily betrothed.

Hand in hand, she and Sterling walked to where the other two were sitting, and Sterling said, 'Here you are, darling,' and pulled up a chair beside his.

'You look charming, Danielle,' Marcus commented with a smile. 'Don't you think so, Lisa?'

'Gorgeous.'

His wife's tone made it perfectly clear that she did not mean what she said. Beside her, Danielle felt awkward and unattractive. In a black and white patterned, mini-skirted dress, with huge white hoops adorning her ears and a black and white bangle on her tanned arm, Lisa looked as if she had stepped from the glossy pages of an expensive fashion magazine.

'Time for a drink,' Marcus said.

For the first time Danielle noticed the bottle resting on a bed of ice in a bucket at Marcus's side. He began to open it with an ease born of long practice.

As he began to pour, Danielle said, 'I think I'll pass up on it, thanks.'

Her host lifted an eyebrow. 'You don't drink?'

Refusing to let herself be intimidated, Danielle gave him a smile. 'I enjoy a glass of wine as much as the next person, but this is a bit early in the day for me.'

Lisa laughed the low, husky laugh which put Danielle's teeth on edge every time she heard it. 'You've found yourself a bit of a prude, Sterling. Isn't that hard to believe?'

'Now, Lisa, my love, not ours to judge,' remonstrated her husband. 'Danielle, won't you reconsider? This isn't wine, it's champagne, and it's in your honour. We have to drink to your engagement.'

Champagne... She should have known, of course: there had been the pop of the cork before it sailed across the patio, alighting in one of the big clay tubs.

Sterling put a hand over hers. 'Marcus is right, darling; we should be celebrating.'

That word again. Loathing the sham, Danielle wished that the warmth of Sterling's touch weren't quite so exciting.

'Silly of me; I should have realised we were celebrating,' she said lightly, and took a glass from Marcus.

'To Sterling and his very beautiful fiancée, and may they spend a life of happiness together,' Marcus toasted.

There was a mutual clinking of glasses, and then Sterling leaned towards Danielle. He linked his arm through hers, and they drank the sparkling liquid.

She was about to withdraw her arm when Sterling leaned even closer. 'I echo the sentiments of our host,' he said softly. His free hand cupped Danielle's chin, holding her firm as he kissed her. The kiss seemed to last for ever, but at last Sterling drew away from her. For a long moment his gaze held hers, his expression infinitely disturbing. Yet when he faced their hosts once more there was a sparkle in his eyes.

'Thanks for the nice words, Marcus,' he said.

They sipped their champagne and made animated small talk—at least, the other three talked; Danielle was largely silent—and then Lisa looked at her without warning and said, 'Have we met?'

Danielle stared at her in amazement. On that fateful day in Sterling's office Lisa had turned her head just as Danielle had beat a very hasty retreat. It seemed unlikely that she could have seen Danielle for more than a second or two—certainly not long enough to remember her face.

'I beg your pardon?' she responded slowly, giving herself time to think.

'You look vaguely familiar, and yet I can't place you.'

Involuntarily, Danielle glanced at Sterling, but this time there was no expression in the eyes that met hers. So there was to be no direction from that quarter, she thought grimly.

'We've never been introduced,' she told Lisa truthfully.

'Are you sure?'

'Positive.'

'Well, maybe not. And yet I could swear I've seen you somewhere.' Lisa slung back another half-glass of champagne. 'Never mind, it will come to me; I never forget a face.'

Sterling grinned at her. 'Hardly worth losing your beauty sleep over.'

To which Lisa gave him a languidly seductive look. 'Very little gets in the way of that. But to get back to the two of you—how did you get together?'

'Now there's a story—we'll have to tell it to you some time,' Sterling said easily.

'Now's as good a time as any.'

But Sterling just grinned at her again.

Lisa made a mock pout. 'OK, then, *when* did you meet? You can't have known each other very long.'

'You're making Danielle feel uncomfortable,' her husband said.

'Nonsense, Marcus. Really, Sterling...Danielle...I'm interested in this engagement. Must have been a whirlwind affair—was it? I mean, it's not as if the two of you were seeing each other.'

'How would you know that, Lisa, my angel?' There was another dose of malice in Marcus's voice.

So he did know about Lisa and Sterling, Danielle thought. Or perhaps he was only guessing. She was beginning to feel distinctly embarrassed.

But if Lisa was in any way upset about being caught off her guard her expression did not reveal it. 'Why wouldn't I know? Word gets around. The trusty grapevine never fails; affairs of the heart don't stay secret for long.' She turned once more to Danielle. 'You can't have known Sterling long. No more than a—' This time she managed to catch herself in time. 'How can you possibly be engaged?'

'How about love at first sight?' Sterling's eyes were dark with mischief as he reached for one of Danielle's hands and placed it against his cheek in a playfully intimate gesture.

'Give me a break, Sterling!'

'No, really. Sometimes people don't need much time. Not when they both know what they want the moment they set eyes on each other. Isn't that right, darling?'

It had been that way with Danielle. Even now, the roughness of his cheek against her palm filled her with sensations that were impossible to ignore. She had to remind herself that Sterling's tenderness was nothing but a game.

She managed a hoarsely muttered yes, after which she drew her hand out of Sterling's and let it fall back on her lap. Watching as Lisa slung back another glass of champagne, she wondered whether the alcohol had gone to the other woman's head. Why else would she persist in asking such dangerously indiscreet questions in the presence of her jealous husband?

Ever urbane, Marcus was smiling once more. 'Love at first sight—so that's what it was. How sweet. Don't you think so, Lisa, my pet?'

'Nauseatingly so,' his wife responded viciously. 'My God, it's hot!' And, jumping to her feet, she said, 'Why don't we go to the pool before supper?'

When Danielle arrived at the pool twenty minutes later, she found the other three there before her, lying on loungers in the shade. It had taken her a while to decide what to wear—one of the brief new bikinis that Sterling had convinced her to buy or her own one-piece green swimsuit which she had thrown into her case at the last moment. In the end, she had settled for the one-piece.

She saw the way they all looked at her as she took off the matching wrap. Marcus's intensely male gaze lingered with open approval on her long, slim legs; Lisa, wearing a bikini that made even Danielle's new purchases seem prim, looked contemptuous. But it was Sterling's reaction that Danielle sought, and his jawline was hard as he looked at the swimsuit. When his eyes moved up to meet hers, they were shuttered.

To hide her sudden discomfort, Danielle ran to the edge of the pool. She entered the water with a swift, clean dive and swam three lengths without stopping. She was in the deep end, about to start a fourth length, when a pair of strong hands caught her waist and she found herself being pulled up against a hard male body.

'What on earth . . .?' she spluttered.

'Thought I'd join you. You were looking so lovely, I couldn't resist. Where are the new bikinis, Danielle?'

Darting a quick glance at Marcus and Lisa, very close to a tinkling fountain on the other side of the pool, Danielle realised that they could not hear what was being said.

She looked up at Sterling. 'The bikinis? In my room,' she told him saucily.

'Wear one next time, will you?'

The hard body was so close to hers now that a sudden tide of desire swept her. Fighting feelings that threatened to overwhelm her, she tried to push away from Sterling, but he was drawing her ever closer.

'No,' she protested, when his lips were less than an inch from her own.

'Yes,' he insisted, and kissed her.

She tried unsuccessfully to pull away from him. 'That's it! We've done our share of kissing for one day.'

'We haven't done enough.' His breath was warm against her mouth. 'It's what's expected of us; you know that. Engaged couple, whirlwind romance, madly in love. Lisa and Marcus are probably wondering why we're not touching all the time we're together.'

'I can't bear this, Sterling,' she said wildly.

'Poor Danielle,' he mocked. 'You'll just have to try, won't you?'

With which he bent his head towards her once more.

'No, Sterling!' she hissed. 'I mean it. Even for a genuinely engaged couple, we've had enough. Besides, I hate being watched.'

'That's the point of this exercise.'

'Exercise?'

'Your performance earlier was pathetic, to say the least. Your lukewarm reaction to me on the patio, when we were supposed to be celebrating our engagement ... The most priggish of people would have had to wonder whether you were really in love.'

'It was the best I could do,' Danielle protested tensely.

'On the contrary,' Sterling said lazily, 'I happen to know you can do better. I haven't forgotten how passionate you really are. I know you haven't forgotten either.'

Danielle felt a little ill. 'What happened in Hawaii is in the past. It was over long ago.'

Sterling's expression hardened. 'You may be right about that. The fact is, you're here to play a part and you're going to play it properly.'

'No,' Danielle said desperately.

'If we're going to convince the Renfields that we're really in love, you're going to have to perform a lot better than you've done until now.'

'I can't do it!'

'Sure you can,' Sterling said. 'However, just in case you've really forgotten, I'm about to show you how.'

She tried to back away from him, but his arms had already tightened around her. And then he was kissing her with all the ardour she remembered. In seconds the familiar hunger wakened to flaming life. Danielle forgot that what was happening was just an exercise. The only reality was the fact that she was in love with this man.

Her back arched, and her head tilted so that she could kiss him more fully. She felt the hiss of his warm breath against her lips, and then he was exploring her willing mouth, covering every inch of her face and throat with kisses.

She was weak with sensation, ready to do anything he asked of her, when his head lifted and he said, 'I knew you could do it.'

The words struck Danielle with the force of a brutal physical blow. In that moment she was oblivious of the watching Renfields. Desperate to hurt Sterling as he had hurt her, she raised a hand in the direction of his face.

In an instant he had caught the hand, forcing it down before it could reach its target. 'Don't be an idiot!' he ground out fiercely. 'Do you want to ruin everything?'

'Let me go, Sterling! Out of the pool. Away from this place.'

'We have a deal,' he reminded her.

A picture of the red-roofed house flashed momentarily before her eyes. She and Toby needed their own home—but was it worth any expense?

'I never thought it would be like this...' she said wildly. 'Never realised... It can't be too late to back out.'

'It is too late,' Sterling told her firmly. As if to reinforce his words, he kissed her again.

They sat on the patio before dinner. Afternoon turned to dusk, the western sky awash with pink and gold, and then, quite suddenly, dusk turned to dark.

A million stars studded the sky, shedding a glow over the vineyards and the garden. The cicadas had begun their evening song and the air was fragrant.

As before, Danielle listened while the others talked—talked of people and events in a world that had no connection with her own. A brazen Lisa got in as many loaded comments as she could, each one more outrageous than the last. The men did nothing to deter her; if anything, it seemed to Danielle that they were amused by her rapier thrusts.

Sterling sat close beside Danielle. When his hand reached for hers, she stiffened. But she remembered the part she had contracted to play and left her hand in his.

It grew later and later, and after a while Danielle no longer heard what Lisa said. Breaking a small silence, she looked at the other woman and asked, 'May I use your phone?'

'Sure, go ahead.'

She was walking into the house when she heard Lisa's husky tones. 'Who on earth could she be phoning, Sterling? You must be very sure of your fiancée—or don't you care?'

There was a telephone on a table in the hall. It was so late—they would be wondering why they hadn't heard from her.

'Mommy!' Toby said.

'Did you have a good day, honey?'

'I chased a squirrel.'

'Did you catch it?'

'It got away,' Toby said, so mournfully that Danielle laughed. 'When you coming home, Mommy?'

'As soon as I can, honey.'

'Tomorrow?'

'Not tomorrow. Have you been playing with your firetruck, Toby?'

'Yeah! Grandpa too. We put out some big fires. And Gran made popcorn.'

Such eagerness in his voice. Danielle had only to close her eyes to see Toby's face: the expressive mouth, the soft fair hair, the impish gaze. Sterling's child—in some ways so different from his father, in others so similar.

She couldn't have said what made her turn her head. Sterling was standing in the doorway. It was too dark to see his face.

'I have to go,' she said into the phone.

'But, Mommy—'

'Bye, honey; I'll speak to you again tomorrow.'

With fingers that trembled she put down the receiver. For a few seconds she stood by the telephone, willing herself into composure. Only when she was certain that she could speak calmly did she turn to Sterling.

'Do you make a habit of eavesdropping?'

'Of course not.'

'I heard what Lisa said. I guess you decided to check up on me.'

'You seemed very tense; I wonder why. I only came to see if you were OK.'

'And stayed to listen to my call,' Danielle taunted.

Sterling did not deny it. He took a step towards her. His shoulders were rigid, his expression ominous, his jawline tight.

'I won't be spied on,' Danielle said saucily.

'I suppose you were talking to Toby?'

'Yes. I'll talk to him every day; you can't stop me. In case you're thinking of Marcus and Lisa, you don't have to worry—I'll be discreet.'

The evening ended at last. Danielle allowed Sterling, her outwardly devoted fiancé—what a fine actor he was!— to walk her to her room. Luckily, the Renfields were not around to see them, so a polite goodnight outside the door was enough.

When Danielle was ready for bed, she hung the clothes she had worn that day in her wardrobe. She was about to close the door when something drew her eyes. Puzzled, she looked closer, only to let out an exclamation of amazement and outrage.

The black dress! The strapless dress with the slit up the thigh, which Sterling had paid for and which Danielle had refused to pack. The seductive dress she had sworn never to wear. It was hanging between her other clothes. Her fingers shook as she touched it.

What was the dress doing in her wardrobe?

CHAPTER SIX

BY NINE o'clock the next morning, Danielle was at the pool—by herself this time. Sterling and Marcus were already deep in discussion; of Lisa, thankfully, there had been no sign until now.

What a relief to be able to enjoy a swim on her own! Several lengths of quick crawl, and then she turned on her back. Eyes closed, she floated, enjoying the buoyant water and the warmth of the sun.

At the sound of footsteps she unwillingly opened her eyes, to see Lisa stopping at the edge of the pool, her sinuous body almost naked in a bikini that was, if possible, even skimpier than the one she had worn the previous day. Dipping one foot fastidiously into the water, she shuddered, then looked at Danielle with a mixture of hostility and dislike.

Danielle dropped her own feet to the floor of the pool.

'Hi.' She tried to make the greeting friendly.

'Hi. Where are the men?'

'In Marcus's den.'

'What are they doing?'

'Talking.'

'Discussions, discussions. So tiresome.' With a heavy sigh, Lisa sat down on a lounger, took out a bottle of suntan lotion, and began to oil herself.

The joy had gone out of swimming. Reluctantly, Danielle climbed out of the pool. She saw Lisa's sour expression as she reached for her towel, and suddenly she was glad that she had decided to wear one of her new bikinis. She had been in two minds about it at first, part of her wanting to annoy Sterling by wearing the more modest one-piece, another part eager to prove that her body was every bit as attractive as that of her hostess.

And the jade bikini did just that. It exposed the swell of her breasts and made her legs look even longer and slimmer than usual; it deepened the colour of her eyes, the sheen of her hair and the pale honey shade of her skin.

When she had towelled herself dry, she settled herself not far from Lisa. Every instinct urged her to distance herself from her hostess, but she did not want to give Lisa the satisfaction of having sent her scurrying.

'You've no idea how much I hate those endless discussions,' Lisa went on. 'I *adore* the money Marcus earns, and the luxuries it can buy me, but I couldn't care less about the ins and outs of the hotel and wine industries. Or any other business for that matter.'

'Whereas I,' Danielle said, 'find the business world interesting.'

'You don't say.' Lisa sounded bored. 'Know much about it?'

'A little, and learning more all the time.'

'Learning from Sterling?' The question was casually put.

Danielle hesitated. She was on dangerous territory now: if she wasn't careful she might say something that would make an already suspicious Lisa even more so, thereby wrecking the charade that Sterling had so carefully concocted. It deserved to be wrecked, she thought grimly.

'Sterling—and others,' she said lightly.

'The two of you must have such wonderfully fascinating conversations. Funny that; I mean, knowing Sterling as well as I do...' Lisa paused to let the words make an impact '...I can't imagine him talking business when he's with a woman.' She gave a grating laugh. 'But then that's just one of the things that puzzles me about your so-called relationship.'

'So-called?' Danielle repeated evenly.

'Your engagement—for want of a better word.'

Danielle applied a little oil to her face, then put on large sunglasses. Besides shielding her eyes from the glare of the water, they would conceal her reactions from Lisa—a necessary precaution, since she guessed that the other woman was out to bait her.

'I'm not sure what you mean,' she said carefully.

'Oh, come on!' Lisa made an impatient gesture. 'We all know there's something very weird about the whole set-up.'

'Do we?'

'It's obvious. Love at first sight! I've never heard of anything so ridiculous!'

'You don't think people can fall in love the moment they lay eyes on each other?' Danielle was glad of her dark glasses.

'The words Sterling used yesterday—did you rehearse them beforehand?'

Danielle was shaken, but she managed to hide it. 'Why would we do that? But about love at first sight—you don't believe it can happen?'

'To some people, perhaps, but not Sterling Tenassik. And certainly not with you, Danielle.'

'Thanks for the compliment.'

Again that unpleasant laugh. 'Sarcasm is lost on me, so don't bother with it. Look, Danielle, I know there's something phony about the engagement; I knew it the moment I saw you together. And I'm more convinced than ever now.'

'Why?' Danielle couldn't help being genuinely curious. Sterling had seemed so certain that the Renfields would be taken in by their act. How could he have been so wrong?

'Well, for one thing, if you were really in love with the guy you'd want to share a room. You'd insist on it. These are the nineties, for heaven's sake; Marcus was right—everybody takes living together for granted. And don't hand me that cute stuff about being old-fashioned; I don't believe it for a moment.'

'Why not?'

'If you were old-fashioned you wouldn't be wearing that bikini; you'd have stuck with the swimsuit. Know what I think, Danielle?'

'What?' Danielle asked, knowing that Lisa would tell her anyway.

'You don't care about sex.'

'Really?' A deliberately light tone concealed the anger that Danielle felt.

'That's right. For reasons known only to yourself, you want Sterling, but you don't want to sleep with him. Poor Sterling—he may actually believe all that garbage about your being old-fashioned. I pity him; he's in for a shock when you're married and he finds out the truth.'

Danielle was growing angrier by the moment. 'That's some conclusion,' she said evenly.

'The correct one, I'm willing to bet. There's the way you kiss, for one thing. I've been watching you. Prim little miss letting her man touch her lips under duress. Oh, sure, things hotted up in the pool yesterday—briefly—but I sensed that was only because Sterling was egging you on. It wasn't what you wanted.'

She would have to watch herself in Lisa's company, Danielle realised: the woman was frighteningly perceptive.

'Not much passion in you, is there, Danielle?'

'It's none of your business.'

Lisa laughed contemptuously. 'Your fiancé likes passion; take it from me that he does. He's a sexy guy—in case you haven't noticed—and he adores beautiful, sexy women. That man thrives on excitement. I don't know what he sees in you, but I'm certain it won't last. For some bizarre reason he's attached to you now, but you're not his type—how can you be? You're too quiet, too timid. You're so boringly ordinary.'

Danielle's nails dug painfully into the soft palms of her hands. 'Are you always so rude?'

HOW TO PLAY
£ SIX HUNDRED THOUSAND
BIG BUCKS
£ SIX HUNDRED THOUSAND
AND YOU COULD WIN THE
£600,000
PLUS JACKPOT!
YOUR *PERSONAL* GAME CARD INSIDE...
Mills & Boon®

THE £600,000 PLUS JACKPOT!

IT'S FUN! IT'S FREE!

3 HARLEQUIN ENTERPRISES LTD.

TWO WAYS TO WIN BIG BUCKS!

1. Uncover 5 '£' signs in a row... BINGO!
You're eligible to win the £600,000 PRIZE DRAW!

2. Uncover 5 '£' signs in a row AND '£' signs in all 4 corners... BINGO!
You're eligible to win the £30,000 EXTRA BONUS PRIZE!

LUCKY CHARM GAME!

Claim up to 4 FREE books AND a FREE Mystery Gift!

HURRY This jackpot must be claimed! Scratch here

YES! I have played my Big Bucks game card as instructed. Enter my Big Bucks Prize number in the £600,000 Prize Draw and enter me for the Extra Bonus Prize. When the winners are selected, tell me if I've won. If the Lucky Charm is scratched off, I will also receive everything revealed, as explained on the back and on the opposite page. *I am over 18 years of age.*

10A6N

Ms /Mrs/Miss/Mr _____ BLOCK CAPITALS PLEASE

Address _____

_____

_____ Postcode _____

mps MAILING PREFERENCE SERVICE

You may be mailed with offers from other reputable companies as a result of this application. If you would prefer not to share in this opportunity please tick box. ☐

EXCLUSIVE PRIZE Nº

C:07451

BIG BUCKS

3

Book offer closes 30th April 1997. All orders subject to approval. * Prices and terms subject to change without notice. All orders subject to approval. * Offer valid in UK and Ireland only. Book offer limited to one per household and is not available to current subscribers to this series. **Readers in Ireland please write to: P.O. Box 4546, Dublin 24.** Overseas readers please write for details.

THE READER SERVICE: HERE'S HOW IT WORKS

Accepting free books places you under no obligation to buy anything. You may keep the books and gift and return the invoice marked "cancel". If we don't hear from you, about a month later we will send you 6 additional books and invoice you for just £2.10* each. That's the complete price, there is no extra charge for postage and packing. You may cancel at any time, otherwise every month we'll send you 6 more books, which you may either purchase or return - the choice is yours.

* Prices and terms subject to change without notice.

The Reader Service
FREEPOST
Croydon
Surrey
CR9 3WZ

NO
STAMP
NEEDED

'Always. Just as you're always so tediously polite. Give me rudeness any day; it's more interesting, and it doesn't bore a man out of his mind. Thing is, Danielle, any woman worth her salt would be fighting back right now, giving as good as she got.'

'You and I have different styles, Lisa.'

'You can say that again! But about Sterling . . . Aren't you going to ask me how I know so much about him?' Lisa's eyes sparkled with venom.

'I would if I was interested. As it happens, I'm not.'

'God, you're so prim, it's really nauseating,' Lisa mocked. 'I'll tell you anyway. *I* am Sterling's type.'

Lisa's cheeks were flushed now, her eyes too bright, her mouth contorted in a smile that was anything but pleasant. 'Sterling and I have been very good friends for some time,' she continued with undisguised satisfaction. *'Extremely good friends.'*

The same words that Sterling had used. Danielle managed a careless shrug.

'Do I have to spell that out, Danielle?'

'Hardly. I get your drift.'

'And you're not bothered?'

'Why should I be?' Danielle looked pointedly at her ring. 'I'm engaged to Sterling, Lisa, not you.'

'You *say* you're engaged, and you're wearing that rock to prove it. Still—' Lisa frowned '—I don't believe it. It doesn't make any sense. For one thing, I know quite positively that Sterling couldn't be attracted to you. As for the idea of a whirlwind romance—that's absurd.' She sat up. 'Sterling never did say—how did the two of you meet?'

'I'm not in the mood to talk about it.'

'I want to know.' For a woman who was supposed to be sophisticated, Lisa could sometimes sound unbelievably childish and petulant. 'I asked questions yesterday but there weren't any answers. How long have you known each other? And what's it really all about, this love-at-first-sight thing?'

'It's personal.' Danielle's voice was low.

'Another polite way of telling me to mind my own business. Clam up all you like, but I know there's a reason for your engagement.' Her eyes went quite blatantly to Danielle's stomach. 'Are you pregnant?'

'I am not,' Danielle responded tightly.

'Of course, you can't be—you don't even share a bed. How could I forget? So it's not a baby. All the same, something very strange is going on here, and I mean to find out what it is.'

Danielle stood up and slipped on her sandals. She was about to walk away when Lisa said, 'One other thing.'

'I've heard enough.'

'For your own sake, I think you should hear this.' Lisa's tone oozed poison. 'What Sterling and I have together will continue. Understand that, Danielle. We'll always be lovers. Our relationship will go on; it won't change with your marriage.' She paused a moment. When she went on, her voice was huskier than before, and even more poisonous. 'Sterling will never admit it to you, of course. In fact, if you were to tell him about our conversation he'd be very angry. He can't stand a jealous woman.'

'You're trying to intimidate me, Lisa. That's what all this is about.'

The other woman gave a sultry laugh. 'Why on earth would I do that? I have an elderly and extremely rich husband who worships the ground I walk on and gives me everything I could possibly want. And I have a young, virile, sexy "friend" who provides for me in other ways. The best of two worlds, and it's the way I like it. Go ahead and talk to Sterling, Danielle, why don't you? I can tell you exactly how he'll react. At best, he'll deny the whole thing. At worst, if you're stupid enough to make a scene and try to saddle him with a guilt trip, he might even call off the engagement.'

'You're a cruel woman,' Danielle said slowly.

'Cruel? Actually, you could say I'm kind; I'm doing you a favour. At least, I'm warning you beforehand that nothing will change after your marriage—*if you do in fact get married*. I'd have thought you'd want to know that.'

'Feel like a walk, Danielle?' Sterling asked the next day.

Eyes brightening, she accepted the invitation with alacrity.

'Sweet,' Lisa mocked. 'The about-to-be-marrieds sneaking off by themselves. Remember what it was like to be madly in love, Marcus, honey?'

'I may, you don't, Lisa. You've never loved anyone but yourself,' responded her husband equably.

Lisa greeted the brutal comment with her trademark husky laugh. Glancing at her, Danielle wondered if she was the only one to pick up the fact that the other woman was distinctly unamused. Her face had a tight, angry look.

Danielle let Sterling take her hand as they left the patio and walked across the garden. Vineyards lay beyond the garden on three sides, extending all the way to the horizon and far beyond. On the fourth side was a stretch of wild woodland; it was in that direction that they were now walking.

'Quite a spring in your step.' Sterling sounded amused.

Danielle danced him a grin. 'It's a relief to get away from that house for a while.'

'Lisa giving you a hard time?'

The grin vanished. Mindful of Sterling's relationship with their obnoxious hostess, Danielle confined herself to saying lightly, 'She's not the easiest person in the world to get along with, is she?'

'What has she been saying to you?'

If ever the time was right to tell Sterling the extent of Lisa's cruelty, it was now. For a moment Danielle was tempted to let him know exactly what had been said. But the moment did not last. It would not matter to

Sterling that she had been deeply hurt by other woman's taunts. After all, she was being paid very well for her efforts, and Lisa's unkind words came with the territory.

'What has she been saying?' Sterling asked again.

Danielle shrugged. 'No more than I'd expect from her.'

'I take it you don't like Lisa.'

'You don't really want to know how I feel about her.'

'I wouldn't ask if I didn't.'

'OK, then. Lisa is . . . very beautiful. She's also hard and cold and insensitive.' Danielle turned her head to look at Sterling. 'Sorry, but you did ask. I guess I've hurt your feelings. I could have been more diplomatic and told you a polite social lie.'

Sterling's eyes glittered. 'Lisa has a husband.'

'I'm surprised to hear you acknowledge the fact.'

'Is that right?' he responded blandly.

'A husband—and a lover.'

'Would you believe me if I said I haven't been sleeping with her?'

'Since we've been here—is that what you mean? There hasn't been an opportunity, has there? Besides, even if I were not around, there's always Marcus.'

'In fact, Lisa and I—'

'I don't want to hear about it,' Danielle interrupted him sharply.

'Are you certain?'

'Quite.'

'Danielle—'

'Talking of Marcus—' she was desperate to lead the subject away from Lisa '—I feel sorry for him, but he's also intimidating.'

'Is that the effect he has on you?'

'You're all so sophisticated, Sterling. Worldly. So different from the kind of people I'm used to.'

'Poor Danielle.' To her chagrin, Sterling was laughing. 'Have I asked a lot of you by bringing you here?'

'You know you have; though, considering the huge salary you're paying me, I guess I shouldn't complain.'

She threw him another sparkling look. 'I hope I'm worth it.'

'Keep working on your performance,' Sterling said drily.

'I've been trying my best.'

'Have you, Danielle?'

'Yes,' she insisted spiritedly. 'But there are things I won't do. Not even for money.'

'Have I asked you to do something so terrible?'

'I think you may be about to.'

Sterling's eyes were bright with laughter. 'Interesting.'

'The black dress.'

One eyebrow lifted. 'I wondered when you'd mention it.'

'You should have listened when I asked you not to buy it. I won't wear it, Sterling; don't ask me to.'

A long thumb moved over her wrist in a way that was almost unbearably sensuous.

'Have you given yourself a chance?' he asked softly.

'What do you mean?' she responded uncertainly.

'Have you taken a proper look at yourself in the dress?'

'Only in the store, and that was enough.'

'Then you must know you were stunning.'

She hesitated a moment. 'I know what I saw in the mirror.'

'What did you see, Danielle?'

'Why ask? You were there; you saw it too.'

'I know what *I* saw.' Sterling's eyes gleamed. 'But it's your reaction that intrigues me. I want to hear you put it into words.'

Danielle managed to face him. Her cheeks were flushed, her eyes stormy. 'I saw a siren,' she told him plainly.

The lines around Sterling's eyes creased with laughter. But there was something else in his expression as well— something suggestive, a little insolent, intoxicatingly seductive. Danielle felt her heart thudding in her chest.

'A siren . . .' he drawled.

'Don't make anything of it.'

'Sirens tempt men,' Sterling said lazily. 'They drive them crazy with desire.'

'Don't—'

'They've been known to change the course of destiny.'

'Stop it!' Danielle was shaking. Abruptly, she pulled her hand from his and stepped away from him.

'Have I said too much for you, Danielle?'

'You make me feel uncomfortable.'

'I'm sorry.'

'You're anything but sorry, Sterling Tenassik! The fact is, you shouldn't have put the dress in my closet. You shouldn't have sneaked into my room when I wasn't about, and you shouldn't—'

'So many shouldn'ts,' he mocked her. 'Would you have put the dress in your closet if I hadn't?'

'Of course not!'

'There you are, then.'

'Why can't I get through to you, Sterling? I told you not to buy the dress. I've already said I won't wear it.'

'You might change your mind.'

'When I decide to change the course of destiny,' she told him tartly.

He laughed at that.

They went on walking. They were in the woods now— a stretch of land which had never been cultivated. The trees grew close together and moss covered the ground and clung to rocks.

Toadstools grew everywhere. Some were large and flat-topped, others were tiny; a few were red-lidded with round white spots.

The black dress forgotten, Danielle was enchanted. 'Those toadstools—straight out of a fairy story. Oh, Sterling, look!'

A tiny frog peeped out from under one of the toadstools, beady eyes fixed on the two humans. When they walked closer, it retreated beneath the protective cover of the toadstool. When they stepped back it moved forward.

'A toad and a toadstool.' Sterling shook with laughter. 'Straight out of your fairy story, Danielle.'

'All you see, Sterling, is a toad.' Her tone was mock-solemn now, but her eyes sparkled.

'Why don't you tell me what I'm missing?'

'The toad is a fairy prince, of course, just waiting for his princess to come along.'

'When she'll change him back into a man,' Sterling finished for her.

They looked at each other, and now they were both laughing. And all at once they were back in that magic time when there had been so much to laugh about.

Sterling was the first to quieten. 'Will the princess come, Danielle?'

'She's there somewhere, lost in all that moss. We can't see her but—' She stopped suddenly, caught by the expression in Sterling's eyes.

'Will she find the way, Danielle?' He spoke in a new tone now—one that was infinitely disturbing.

'Sterling . . .' she said uncertainly.

'Will she, Danielle?'

'Maybe . . .'

'How long will she take? Will she make her man wait long?'

In a moment the blood was racing in Danielle's veins. 'I don't know the answers,' she said bumpily. 'I only know about real life, and that's never the same as a story.'

'It can be,' Sterling said roughly.

And then he was reaching for her.

Danielle closed her eyes as he drew her against him. Hunger stirred inside her.

His lips were just touching hers when she pulled away from him. 'No more kissing,' she whispered.

'Why not?'

'We've done enough kissing the last few days. Far too much. Empty kisses. Phony. They haven't impressed

Lisa; I know because she told me. Heaven only knows if they've fooled Marcus. And they've made me feel ill. You don't know how much I *loathe* what we're doing!'

'We're not trying to fool anyone now, Danielle.' Sterling put his arms out to her once more. 'Nobody can see us.'

'Only the toad, poor thing, which will never turn into a prince,' she said bitterly. Somehow she managed to take a few steps away from Sterling.

'You're trying to say something, Danielle.' His expression had tightened.

'Kissing in front of the Renfields is one thing. I can't like it but I go along with it all the same. The engaged couple, so much in love, unable to keep their hands and lips off each other—all that stuff. Here in the woods... This is something else. There's nobody about to impress.'

'Does that matter, Danielle?' Sterling asked softly.

'Yes.'

'In Hawaii we never needed an excuse to kiss. After those first few days, when we played things slowly, we couldn't bear not to be in each other's arms.'

'I remember...'

'We could never kiss enough.'

'Maybe,' Danielle said painfully, 'it was because we'd set a limit to our kisses. No surnames, no addresses, no strings attached.'

'Danielle—'

'Ten perfect days,' she went on blindly, 'and we had to get in all our kissing before the holiday ended. That was the agreement.'

'You suggested it,' Sterling said in a hard voice.

'And you went along with it. Added to it. Put in conditions of your own.'

'Are you saying that in the end it wasn't what you really wanted?' Sterling's tone was so odd.

Danielle hesitated, but only for a moment. 'We both wanted it.'

Sterling was silent for a while. 'Any reason why we can't pretend we're back in Hawaii?' he asked at length.

'It couldn't work,' Danielle said flatly.

'Why not?'

'What we had then ... It was lovely, Sterling, I don't deny it.'

'It could be lovely again.'

'No, it's over, and we both know it. It's been over a long time.' She swallowed hard over the tears forming in her throat. 'Our kissing is different now. In Hawaii whatever we did was impulsive. Not so here. You need to put on an act for Marcus. And I—' She stopped, drew breath, then said the brutal words. 'I'm doing what I have to because you're paying me so well.'

She stole a glance at Sterling's face; it was paler than it had been, and a little angry. For a while, neither of them spoke. A bird rose from a tree, its cry loud on the silent air. A butterfly hovered over the ground. The toad moved boldly forward, but the humans seemed to have forgotten its existence, and after a few seconds it vanished, unnoticed, between the toadstools.

Sterling broke the silence at last. 'When I tried to kiss you just now, do you think that had anything to do with money?'

'Maybe not.'

'Well, then?' And when she didn't answer he added, 'You enjoyed it once, you could enjoy it again. You couldn't have changed that much, Danielle.'

The tears were in her eyes now; she tried to blink them away. 'It's not just me. Everything has changed.'

'Not quite everything.'

'Yes! And the problem is, I'm having trouble separating the real thing from the act. I can no longer tell the difference between duty and pleasure. You may be able to switch from one to the other with ease, Sterling—I can't do that.' Danielle dashed at a wayward tear before it could trickle onto her cheek.

Sterling cupped her face between his hands. 'Why are you crying?'

She could only stare at him wordlessly.

'Danielle?'

'Give me a break—please; I don't want to talk about it any more,' she whispered. 'Don't you understand?'

Sterling looked down at her for a long moment. His jawline was hard, his eyes deep and shadowed. But not another word passed between them as they turned and walked out of the woods.

They were well away from the trees before they talked again. Instead of going back to the house, Sterling had taken a path that skirted the vineyards. He motioned to Danielle to sit beside him on a sun-warmed rock.

'It was my dream to be a fireman—did you know that, Danielle?'

It was the last thing she'd expected him to say. 'I didn't.' She smiled and made herself say, 'Seems you have something in common with Toby.'

'Seems that way, doesn't it?' He was smiling too. 'I must have been about six at the time, Danielle. We lived near a fire station, and no matter when the bells rang I'd be out of the house like a shot, watching the fire-trucks race along the street. One day there was a fire not far from our home. I remember watching the firemen going about their job. I was enthralled by the hoses, the ladders, the water. From then on I was hooked.'

It was difficult to picture this big, hard-bodied man as a child—a little like Toby, perhaps. Danielle tried and failed. Sterling's legs, tanned and corded with muscle, were much too close to her own. A familiar longing stirred inside her.

'What happened?' she asked.

'My interests were fickle. When I was eight there was a jaunt on a fishing trawler.'

'Let me guess—you were dead keen to become a fisherman after that.'

'Right.' His dark eyes sparkled. 'Other interests followed. Somewhere along the way I came to advertising—'

'And the rest is history,' she finished for him.

He nodded. 'My parents are no longer alive. I have a brother and a sister, both living in different parts of the States. We don't see each other very often, but we have a great time when we do.'

'Why are you telling me all this?' Danielle asked. 'We know very little about each other.'

'That's true... In Hawaii we talked a lot, but never about our personal lives.'

Certain subjects, the ones that really mattered, had been taboo.

'I don't know anything about you, Danielle.'

'I'm an only child. I was a bit of a tomboy when I was young—spent my time swimming and running and climbing every tree I could find. I've always loved drawing and painting. I was going to study art but...'

'But?' Sterling prompted.

Danielle shifted her feet restlessly. 'I had to change my plans.'

'Because of Toby.' It was a statement rather than a question.

Danielle glanced at Sterling, saw the slight tightening of his lips, then glanced away. 'Yes.'

'And a man you've excluded from your life.'

She rose abruptly to her feet. 'The Renfields must be wondering where we are.'

'Concerned about Lisa?' He was looking up at her, his expression sardonic. 'I must have hit quite a nerve.'

'Not the first time you've done that,' Danielle said brusquely.

'You don't want to talk about Toby's father.'

'No, Sterling, I don't.' Her voice shook.

He looked at her a moment longer. And then he was standing up too, and they began walking towards the house.

* * *

There was not a day when Danielle did not speak to her small son. Mostly he sounded happy, but there was also a day when he seemed dejected.

Grandpa was tired, he told her, and Gran was busy. Danielle told Toby she would be back with him soon, but the word 'soon' meant little to a three-year-old and his spirits did not lift when she said it.

'I have to go home,' Danielle told Sterling later that evening, when they were alone.

'Out of the question,' he said, quite pleasantly.

'I *must* go, Sterling.'

'We have an agreement,' he reminded her.

'I haven't forgotten.' Her eyes were distressed. 'It's just that Toby...'

'What about your son, Danielle?'

'He's missing me; he's dispirited. And I miss him too. More than you can possibly imagine.' She looked away from Sterling. 'I know all about our agreement, and I'm not trying to back out of it, but I have to see my child.'

'Our business here isn't finished; we're not ready to leave, Danielle.'

An image of the red-roofed house appeared briefly behind Danielle's eyes. She was under no illusion as to what would happen if she walked out on Sterling: he would not hesitate to punish her for humiliating him; his revenge would be merciless.

'There has to be a way,' she said a little desperately. 'Surely I could take off for a day or two and come back?'

Sterling's eyes gleamed as he regarded her thoughtfully. After a moment he said, 'Better still, I'll go with you.'

Danielle was startled. 'You don't have to do that,' she protested. 'Marcus and Lisa will wonder if you go too.'

His laughter was low and seductive. 'They'll wonder more if I don't. Have you forgotten we're engaged?'

Long before noon the next day they were in San Francisco.

'Mommy!' An excited little boy hurtled frantically down the steps of his grandparents' house and into his mother's outstretched arms.

'Toby! Oh, I've missed you so much, honey.' Danielle was overwhelmed at the sight of her child.

Her parents were delighted to see her. Her father required some post-surgical treatment and her mother wanted to be with him. Some time without Toby to look after was exactly what they needed.

Danielle shot Sterling a pointed look. 'I'll be ready when you come to pick me up the day after tomorrow.'

But Sterling did not go straight to his car as she'd expected. Instead, he looked at Toby. 'How about a picnic, fella?'

'A picnic?' Toby looked intrigued.

'You, your mom and me.'

'Toby and I are going to be spending our time alone.' Danielle did not care if she sounded rude. Sterling had no *right* to intrude upon her precious time with her child.

'We could take a kite,' Sterling said to Toby.

'A kite!' The little boy was excited.

'Danielle?' Sterling looked at her for the first time.

'You leave me little choice,' she said flatly. 'But I do want some time alone with Toby as well.'

The dark eyes laughed at her. 'Tomorrow morning, then? I'll be here around eleven. And don't worry about food; I'll bring whatever we need.'

Danielle's parents had already left by the time the sleek red Porsche stopped outside the house. Danielle was watching through a front window as Sterling got out of the car, a tall, athletic figure, broad-shouldered and powerful in a way that made her heart do a little somersault of pleasure inside her chest.

An hour later they were sitting by a creek some way out of the city, with a picnic basket open beside them. To Danielle's astonishment, she discovered that Sterling had packed a mixed basket of delicacies: crusty dark bread with pâté, artichoke hearts and sun-ripened olives for the two adults; marshmallows, hot dogs and potato crisps for the child. There was even a mixture of drinks: a bottle of wine for Danielle and Sterling, and for Toby a few cans of different-flavoured sodas.

Sterling grinned when he saw Danielle's expression. 'Men do know enough to be able to throw together a bit of food.'

'So I see.' It was hard not to smile back at him. 'All the same, I'm impressed.'

When Sterling had given Toby a bag of crisps and a hot dog, he spread a slice of dark bread with pâté, dropped a few olives on top and handed it to Danielle. 'Enjoy,' he said.

It would have been difficult not to enjoy the interlude—the meal as much as the setting. The picnic scene was idyllic: the clear running water leaping over rounded boulders; a few willows at the water's edge, the tips of their drooping fronds hanging low over the creek; distant mountains; a few wild flowers, heads waving in the breeze. It was a little-known haven of tranquillity well away from the bustle of highways and cities.

They had finished eating when Sterling went to the car and came back with a kite.

Danielle leaned back against a rock as the two males began to explore the mysteries of kite-flying. It quickly became apparent that Sterling was no mean hand at getting a kite to soar skywards with the wind. Young as he was, Toby learned quickly.

Danielle watched them both. Father and son. The father big, supremely certain of himself, dynamic and virile, the son small, eager, his eyes shining with the enjoyment of the game.

Father and son. They looked so *right* together, the silent air carrying their laughter as they ran with the kite.

Tears welled suddenly in Danielle's eyes. Sterling was a man whom any boy would be proud to have as a father, and what a wonderful father he would be. If only his attitude towards commitment were different; if only she could tell him the truth.

When Toby had control of the kite, running along happily with it, Sterling turned towards Danielle. The breath caught in her throat as he came to her. In shorts and a chocolate-coloured T-shirt, he reminded her of the man she had met on the beach in Hawaii. His arms were tanned and corded with hard muscle. His dark hair, blown by the breeze, fell untidily across his forehead, and his eyes—those wonderful dark eyes—sparkled.

The sun was beginning to set when they left the creek. Before long they were back on a highway and merging with the traffic that led back to the city.

'Hungry, Toby?' Sterling asked when they were not far from the house.

'Yeah!'

They stopped at a fast-food restarant—one that catered especially for children—and Toby amazed his mother by devouring another mountain of food. They sat at a small table, close together, looking like a family to any stranger's eye, Danielle thought. Mother, father and the child they had conceived together in a night of abandoned love.

But the love had been one-sided. And they were *not* a family. Never would be. Those were the things she had to remember if her heart was not to break.

Next day, after they had said goodbye to Toby—she *would* be back soon, Danielle had promised her small son—they began the drive back to the vineyard.

For a while the atmosphere in the car was relaxed. Then Sterling said, 'I once helped another boy with a kite.'

'I remember.'

They had been on the beach at the time. A little boy had got his kite-string tangled around a rock and Sterling had freed it for him. Afterwards, Danielle and Sterling had run hand in hand into the water, laughing as they splashed about among the waves, conscious of the desire building inside them both.

'I haven't forgotten anything about that time, Danielle.'

'Don't...' Her throat was tight.

'Why not?'

'I don't want to remember.' Tears hovered once more behind her eyes; it was an effort to blink them back.

A wicked hand left the steering wheel and slid over her thigh. 'We had a good time.'

'We did,' she agreed, her voice bumpy. 'But it's in the past. It's over.'

A little roughly, Sterling said, 'Why do you get so upset whenever I mention Hawaii?'

Danielle tried to move away from the sensuous hand which was making it so difficult to think. 'I...I don't want to talk about it.'

'Why not?' The hand returned to the wheel. When Sterling spoke again his voice was hard. 'Because it meant nothing to you? Is that it? You had a fling, a good old time, and when it was all over you disappeared without stopping long enough to say goodbye. Why, Danielle?'

In seconds Sterling had become Mr Tenassik—cold and arrogant and contemptuous. It was as if the lovely day at the creek had been nothing but a dream.

'There's no point in explaining; you wouldn't understand,' Danielle said dully.

'Maybe I understand a little too well for your comfort.' His voice was like steel. 'You had another man back home, and you wanted no embarrassing holiday reminders turning up to spoil the romance you had going for you in San Francisco. That's it, isn't it, Danielle?'

For a moment she considered telling him that the conclusions he was drawing were wrong and unfair. Then she thought of the alternative. She was not ready to confront Sterling's even greater anger when he understood how close they had come to a commitment that he had never wanted.

Abruptly, Danielle turned her head away from Sterling. As she gazed unseeingly through her window, her tears became more and more difficult to suppress.

'There you are,' Marcus said to Sterling when they arrived at the vineyard. 'I had some new ideas while you were gone. That problem we spoke of a few days ago, and how to handle it—I think I've come up with a solution.'

'Great! I'd like to hear about it.'

'It's complex. I need to get my thoughts sorted on paper before I can give you anything concrete. I've jotted down a few notes but at present they're just a mess of facts and figures. What I need is to get the lot into clearer form. Problem is, I need someone to help me.'

Lisa sighed heavily. 'Sometimes I think you have figures instead of blood filling your veins, Marcus.'

'Don't knock it; it's my business that keep you pampered,' her husband said drily. 'And that's important to you, isn't it, my dear?'

So he was under no illusions as to why Lisa had married him, Danielle thought.

Marcus was looking at Sterling once more. 'I'll have to try and write it all out.'

Impulsively, Danielle said, 'I'll type it for you.'

Her host turned to her in surprise. 'You, Danielle?'

'Didn't Sterling—?' She stopped at the swift pressure of Sterling's fingers on hers. 'I only meant,' she continued more carefully, 'that I could help if you'd let me.'

'Can you type?' Marcus asked.

'Yes. I can also do shorthand or transcribe your notes from a tape, whichever you prefer.'

'Fantastic! Any objections, Tenassik, if we put your fiancée to work for a few hours?'

'The decision is entirely up to Danielle,' Sterling said.

Lisa was silent throughout the exchange. Happening to glance at her once, Danielle noticed the thoughtfulness in her eyes. But her mind was not on Lisa. Not an hour back with the Renfields and already she was beginning to feel restless; far from resenting the idea of doing some work, she actually welcomed it.

Marcus disappeared into the house. When he returned to the patio he had a sheaf of papers in his hand. Sitting down beside Danielle, he began to explain to her what he wanted typed. Did she prefer a word processor or a typewriter? She could have her pick; he had one of each.

Danielle smiled at him. 'A word processor is perfect.'

'We're really in luck, Sterling,' a gratified Marcus said. 'Soon as Danielle gives us what she's typed we can get down to business. It will save us a few days of—'

'I've got it!' Lisa shouted.

The other three stared at her, puzzled. 'We're busy working,' her husband said.

Lisa ignored him. 'I've got it,' she said again. 'I knew all along it was just a matter of time. Remember I said I never forget a face? That it would come to me where I'd seen Danielle?'

Danielle shot a startled glance at an expressionless Sterling, before looking back at Lisa. The woman's eyes glittered with triumph.

'We're in the middle of something important. Is it really necessary to disturb us?' Marcus was clearly more than a little impatient with his wife.

'You don't understand, Marcus; I know who Danielle is. She's one of Sterling's new employees.'

'I'm a secretary,' Danielle acknowledged quietly.

'There! You see! I knew there was something. I must have seen you the day Sterling started work at the company.'

'What,' her husband enquired quietly, 'were you doing there, my love?'

Lisa's cheeks were suddenly brick-red. Her eyes widened as she looked from Sterling to Marcus. The silence was intense.

But Lisa's discomfort did not last long. 'I had something to discuss with Sterling. An idea I needed to run by him. Good grief, I don't live in a cage! I have business ideas all the time, you know that, Marcus, and if I decide to go ahead with something I need to know how to promote it.'

Danielle could only marvel at the ease with which the woman was able to lie. If Marcus did not believe her—and naïve the tycoon was certainly not—he gave no sign of his thoughts.

When he spoke again his tone was level. 'So Danielle is a secretary with Sterling's new company. I fail to see what is so earth-shaking about that.'

'It proves,' Lisa said viciously, 'that I was right all the time. They can't have known each other long. *There is something very fishy about this engagement.*'

CHAPTER SEVEN

'I CAN'T imagine why it took me so long to figure it out.'

Danielle couldn't remember disliking anyone as much as she disliked Lisa. 'Don't you think you're making a big deal of something that really isn't important?' she asked quietly.

The men were closeted in Marcus's den, poring over the notes and schedules which Danielle had typed. Rather than risk another confrontation with Lisa, she had decided not to go to the pool that morning but had retreated with her sketch-pad and pencils to a secluded part of the garden instead. Her heart had sunk when the other woman had tracked her down there.

'It was obvious all along,' Lisa was saying. 'Glaringly so. I must have been blind not to see it. You and Sterling are a couple of idiots if you thought you could keep your secret for long.'

'I don't know what you're getting at.' Danielle wondered how much longer she would be able to keep her temper in check. 'What does it matter if I happen to work at the same company as Sterling? Office romances go on all the time; it's one of the ways people meet.'

'And secretaries marry high-powered executives. Sure, I know that; nobody could ever call me a snob. My point is, not *this* secretary and *this* executive.'

The previous evening, after dinner and several uncomfortable hours in the company of the Renfields, Sterling had come to Danielle's room. Danielle had been all for telling Marcus and Lisa the truth at that point, but Sterling would not hear of it.

And now Lisa was staring at her accusingly. 'The day you arrived, I asked you if we'd met. You said we hadn't.'

'I told you we'd never been introduced,' Danielle said tightly. 'It was perfectly true—we hadn't.'

'But you knew who I was, didn't you?'

Danielle hesitated, just long enough for Lisa to pounce.

'You *did* know! You must have seen me with Sterling. I remember now that you came to his office. I couldn't have seen you for more than a second, but I have a photographic memory for faces. I remember the home-sewn look, everything neat and sensible but not quite professional. Where did all the expensive clothes suddenly come from, Danielle? Did Sterling buy them for you?'

Danielle was growing angrier by the moment. 'Where and how I come by my things doesn't concern you,' she said hotly.

'Question answered,' Lisa said with immense satisfaction. 'Sterling paid the bills.'

'Don't you have more serious things to worry about than my clothes?'

'Such as?'

'The fact that your husband is obviously wondering why you were with Sterling that day.'

'I explained it.' Lisa dismissed the issue airily.

'Not convincingly.'

'Convincingly enough.'

Danielle was curious. 'You don't think Marcus cares that you see other men?'

'Perhaps he does. The fact is—and this is something you will never know yourself, Danielle—when a woman is very beautiful, she can get away with things that other women would never dream of doing.'

'Like having an affair,' Danielle said evenly.

'Quite. Marcus is dazzled by me. He knows I can have any man I choose. Push me too hard and he might just lose me. Of course, I wouldn't really leave him—all that money makes him extremely attractive—but he doesn't know that.'

Danielle was repelled by the extent of Lisa's insensitivity and self-love. 'Fascinating,' she murmured.

'What fascinates *me*, Danielle, is your so-called engagement. You know very well that I was never taken in, not for a second; it was clear all along it couldn't be the real thing. Everything about it was phony from the start.'

'If it was so phony, how do you explain the ring?' Danielle lifted her hand, surprised as always when the sun struck the stone with brilliant light.

'Sterling must have owned it; it's obvious he wouldn't have gone out and bought it. What I don't understand is why he gave it to you.'

'You're welcome to come up with whatever answers you like.' Deliberately, Danielle stood up and began to gather together her possessions.

She was about to walk away when Lisa exclaimed, *'Of course!'* Feeling cold at the certainty in the woman's voice, Danielle stopped in her tracks.

'Darling Sterling, he thought the whole thing up. Clever, clever Sterling.'

Danielle suppressed an icy shiver. 'What on earth are you talking about now?'

'He needed a way to come here, to talk business with Marcus without making the rich old dear jealous and suspicious. It was always possible that Marcus might have heard rumours about us. And so Sterling hit on the idea of an engagement.' Lisa clapped her hands. 'God, what an idea! *Brilliant! Utterly brilliant!* With that incredible rock of a ring on your finger, Sterling and I can carry on a relationship right under Marcus's nose.'

'You've got it all worked out, haven't you, Lisa?'

'It's falling into place. You're nothing but a smokescreen, Danielle.'

'A smokescreen . . . How flattering.'

'Don't sound so put out. There's sure to be a man for you out there somewhere. But not my Sterling. Remember me telling you that you aren't his type?'

'Evidently it's never occurred to you that he might find me attractive.'

Lisa laughed her husky laugh. 'Attractive? You? You're joking, aren't you? A modest, prim, conservative, neatly dressed little grey mouse. A competent secretary but so boring. Sterling is hot for *me*, Danielle. In a million years he'd find nothing in you. Even with all the most expensive clothes, you still have no sex appeal.'

Anger was red and hot now, filling Danielle's mind, burning her chest, consuming every fibre of her being. She had never in all her life been quite so angry.

'How did he get you to do it?' Lisa grabbed her arm, long red nails biting into her soft skin.

'Let go of me!' Danielle spat.

'Did he pay you?' And as Danielle's cheeks flooded with sudden colour she cried, 'That's it! He paid you. Beautiful! Absolutely beautiful! That explains the separate rooms, of course. How much did you get him to shell out? Not that I blame you—we all have to take as much as we can get.' The fingers tightened. 'What happens when you leave here, little mouse? The ring goes back to Sterling, but what happens to the rest of the things? Do you get to keep the clothes or do they go back to the expensive boutiques?'

Danielle yanked her arm out of the other woman's vicious grip. Without a word she strode away. Lisa's laughter rang out behind her, but this time she did not look back.

Entering the house, she went straight to her room. Standing at the window, she gazed unseeingly over the manicured garden with its profusion of lovely flowers and shrubs. She was still very angry but at least her mind had cleared somewhat. For the first time since listening to Lisa's poison she was able to think.

*   *   *

A dab of exotic perfume behind each ear, another dab between her breasts. A last look in the mirror. A deep, calming breath.

Danielle left the room, closing the door firmly behind her, and began to make her way slowly down the stairs. From the living-room came the sound of animated voices, a sultry laugh, the clatter of glasses. Twice already Sterling had come to call her. The Renfields were having a party and most of the guests had arrived. Danielle had told him to go on without her.

At the entrance to the living-room she paused. People were gathered in groups. Marcus, suave and distinguished as usual, was standing by the fireplace, drink in hand, expounding on some point to a few of his guests. Sterling and Lisa were side by side on a two-seater settee. Sterling was leaning towards Lisa, lighting a cigarette for her, and her hand was curled around his in what might have been taken as an innocent gesture, although Danielle knew it to be a seductively intimate one.

Nobody noticed the figure standing silently in the doorway, nervously observing the lively scene. There was a moment when Danielle's courage almost failed her, when she was on the point of turning tail and retreating to her room. And then she thought of Lisa and her vicious taunts, and she stepped away from the doorway and into the room.

Marcus saw her first. His eyes widened in astonishment; his mouth dropped. *'Danielle!'* he exclaimed, and in a moment he was moving towards her.

Conversation around the room died away. There was a buzz of whispers; Danielle caught the words *'Who is she?'*

And then Sterling's head turned. He looked no less stunned than Marcus. Shaking off Lisa's hand, he was on his feet in an instant, and then he too was going towards Danielle. Lisa stayed where she was—a subdued Lisa, Danielle noted—her face a mask of furious incredulity.

'You look incredible,' Marcus said. 'What will you have to drink, my dear?' His hand cupped Danielle's elbow in an intimate fashion as he led her into the room.

Danielle suppressed a smile. Marcus was always the perfect host but she had never seen him quite so attentive.

Sterling was on her other side now. As Marcus left them in order to fetch Danielle a drink, Sterling murmured, 'A lovely siren. Quite a transformation.'

She smiled up at him, happy that he had remembered the word, that he was turning it into a private joke.

'A transformation you like?' she asked softly.

'Need you ask? "Like" is an understatement. In that dress—I thought you'd never wear it—you're the stuff dreams are made of. Sexy, seductive, infinitely desirable... luring any man you please to the destiny of your choice.'

'What nonsense you talk.'

'Look around you, Danielle; there's not a man who's not totally bowled over by you.'

Beyond his shoulder she could see Lisa, pouting and enraged. She laughed up at Sterling. 'Do you mean that?'

'I mean it when I tell you that I would like to make love to you—right now, very passionately. That I would like to keep you in my bed all night.'

'Oh, really?' she said a little breathlessly.

'Better believe it. Let's go to my room, Danielle.'

'You know that we can't. What would Marcus think?' She was smiling, but her voice was unsteady.

'He'd be envying me intensely, as would every other man here. But you're right—we have to stay; we'd be missed. Have to wait till this evening is over.'

'Danielle...' Marcus was back with her drink. The private moment with Sterling was at an end.

A little later, on her way into the dining-room for dinner, Danielle caught an unexpected glimpse of herself in a gilt-edged mirror.

If anything, the black dress was even more devastatingly seductive than it had appeared in the fitting-room of the boutique. The strapless bodice fitted snugly, emphasising her creamy throat and shoulders, lifting and moulding her softly rounded breasts. The slit revealed the extent of a long, shapely leg. The dress was a masterpiece: clinging, revealing, promising, inviting, yet creating an aura of mystery at the same time.

But the dress was only one part of Danielle's transformation. She had swept up her fair curls on the back of her head, leaving only a few soft tendrils to escape across her forehead and behind her ears. Her make-up was more liberal than usual, but subtly applied. Her eyes were huge and lustrous, her cheekbones high, the curve of her lips delicate.

'A girl in a portrait.' Marcus was making no attempt to hide his admiration.

'Cinderella dressed up for the ball,' Lisa countered. Sourly she added, 'Forgetful of the fact that the attention of the prince is only temporary, and that it's just a matter of time before her coach turns into a pumpkin.'

Danielle saw the disapproving glance that Marcus threw his wife. She also saw the sparkle of delighted amusement in Sterling's eyes.

After dinner there was dancing in the living-room. When Marcus had put on some music, he came to Danielle and said, 'May I?'

As she went into his arms, she heard Lisa inviting Sterling to dance with her. Marcus held Danielle a little too tight, but without making a scene it would have been difficult to discourage him. Lisa's arms had gone around Sterling's neck, but incredibly Danielle did not mind. The attention she had been receiving all evening had gone to her head even more than the wine she had drunk. She felt giddy with excitement and pleasure.

One man after another asked her to dance. She had never been so popular.

At last Sterling prised himself loose from the clinging Lisa and said, 'My turn.' A reluctant partner released Danielle and she went into Sterling's arms.

For a while the music had been lively, but now it was slow. Sterling moved his legs sensuously, deliberately against Danielle's, and she made no attempt to dissuade him. Her blood was liquid fire in her veins, and her heart beat so hard against her ribs that she thought Sterling must surely feel it, but the knowledge did not upset her. This was one evening when absolutely nothing could upset her.

Now and then she was aware of Lisa watching her, and she saw the hatred in the other woman's expression. At another time she might have felt apprehensive. But not tonight—tonight she laughed right back into Lisa's face.

The evening ended. Marcus, dancing with Danielle one last time, caught her to him and, before a startled Danielle could protest, kissed her on the lips. Having said their farewells, the guests drove away into the night. Marcus and Lisa went off in the direction of their bedroom, and Sterling and Danielle made for the guest wing.

Every evening until now, at Danielle's insistence, Sterling had said goodnight to her outside her room. 'I'm coming in,' he told her this time as they approached the door. 'And don't even try fighting me on this.'

The evening had been perfect. Still drunk on flirtatiousness and fun, attention and wine, Danielle did not have the will to fight him. Tonight everything was different. She was smiling as she stepped aside and let him in.

Sterling took her in his arms, as she had known he would, and held her against him for several seconds. His body was long and hard, just as she remembered it from the good times. His lips moved in her hair. Danielle let herself lean against him—just this one time, she told herself—and closed her eyes. She did not try to suppress the emotions that threatened to overwhelm her, or the knowledge that she loved this man so deeply that she would never love anyone else.

She did not resist when he carried her to a chair, sat down and drew her onto his lap.

'Now,' he said, 'are you going to tell me what that was all about?'

'You're asking about the dress . . .'

'The one you *swore* you would never wear. And more than the dress. The alluring hairstyle. The perfume that was designed with the express purpose of driving a sane man out of his mind. You saw the effect you had on our host. And you dazzled me, my darling Danielle.'

Darling . . . Said in privacy for once. Her pulses leaped.

'Why?' His face was so close to hers that his breath was warm on her cheeks.

'When a woman wears a party dress, does there have to be a reason?' she asked, deliberately playing for time.

'This dress? This woman? Yes.'

Danielle shifted on his lap and his arm tightened around her. 'Don't move; this feels just right.'

It felt more than 'just right'—it felt wonderful, Danielle thought.

'Well, Danielle?'

She would have liked to remain sitting like that always. Not talking. Just delighting in the feel of his body. Recapturing some of the magic she'd thought was gone for ever.

But Sterling wanted to talk. He was waiting for her answer.

'Lisa,' Danielle said slowly.

'I had a feeling she had a part in it somewhere.'

'She knows, Sterling.'

'She knows you're my secretary.'

'She knows a lot more than that. Everything, in fact.'

'Is that so?' Oddly, Sterling did not sound the least bit disconcerted.

'She worked it all out. The expensive clothes. The ring—do you know, she actually believes it's a real diamond? She even told me the reason for our engagement. Our "so-called" engagement, as she insists on calling it.'

'And that upset you?'

'I felt cheap and ashamed—not for the first time since we started this charade.'

'Angry?'

'Burningly,' Danielle said after a moment. 'I don't know if you can understand.'

'Why wouldn't I?'

'You might think all that lovely money you're paying me should take care of my emotions.'

'It doesn't?' He asked so oddly.

'It does not!' Danielle hotly. 'Whatever you may think about me—whatever Lisa thinks—I'm a person. Yes, I had a price—*I wish I hadn't*—but it doesn't alter the way I think and feel and act.'

'Of course not.'

Danielle was taken aback. After a moment she said, 'Does that mean you understand?'

'Partly. You haven't told me about the dress.'

'Yes, well...' She was beginning to feel a little foolish. 'You don't really want to hear this.'

Sterling's eyes gleamed. 'Don't leave anything out.'

Reluctantly, she told him about Lisa's taunts—about her fury at being called a modest, prim, conservative, neatly dressed little grey mouse.

Sterling began to laugh. 'So that's it! You decided to prove Lisa wrong.'

'I had to.'

'And so the "prim little mouse"—Lisa's words, not mine, Danielle—transformed herself into a stunningly beautiful, exciting and desirable woman.'

'You're saying I succeeded?'

'You don't need me to tell you that, surely? You had every man in the house running circles around you.'

'Because of the dress...'

'Not the dress, Danielle, though that was a small part of it. It was because of the woman inside it. The dress only showed her as she really is.'

Danielle was still doubtful. 'Lisa said I have no sex appeal.'

Sterling shook with laughter. 'Little does she know!'

'Do I, Sterling?'

He folded his arms around her in such a way that her face was against his. Beneath her, his legs were hard and exciting.

'Don't you know, Danielle?' His voice was rough.

'I know that when you kiss me you're putting on an act for Marcus.'

'I wasn't putting on an act four years ago.'

'Sterling—'

'The passion. The excitement. The bliss of being together. You remember it all.'

'I do.' Her tone was low. 'Both of us getting over our own particular unhappiness, in the mood for re-assurance, hungry for some fun.'

'You're saying you only came to me on the rebound?'

Danielle hesitated a moment, feeling the sudden tension in his arms. 'I'm saying that what we had was a holiday romance. One that suited us both.' He would never know how much it hurt her to say those words.

'Did you ever think it could be more than that, Danielle?'

There was the strangest note in his tone. A warning? Danielle wondered.

She levered herself off his lap. As matter-of-factly as she could, she said, 'Of course not. We both had our reasons for not wanting the relationship to continue. That was why we made the agreement.'

'Right.' Sterling's voice had turned to ice.

The delicious, giddy feeling that had been with her all evening was gone in an instant. All at once Danielle felt a little ill. 'I...I think you should go,' she said unsteadily.

Sterling looked at her. 'You do know that I came here to kiss you?'

'Yes.'

'To make love to you?'

Her heart did a little somersault, then was still. 'I thought we'd agreed to keep our... our kisses for public performance only.'

'It doesn't have to be that way, Danielle.'

'It's the only way I know at this point.'

'Still having trouble distinguishing between reality and pretence?'

'I'm afraid so.'

In a second he was on his feet. Before she could move away from him, his arms were around her and he was drawing her close. His kisses were hard, passionate— and angry. When he released her, quite abruptly, his eyes were angry as well.

At the door of the room he turned back. 'Something for you to remember,' he said tightly. 'Never go out of your way to inflame a man if you have no intention of carrying through on your promises.'

'Sterling—'

'Goodnight, Danielle.'

It wasn't until noon the next day that they were all together again. The men had spent the morning closeted in Marcus's den. Danielle, in no mood to be alone with Lisa, had taken her sketch-pad to a remote field with a lovely view of the distant hills.

They met for lunch. A sense of anticlimax pervaded the house, and, somewhat to Danielle's surprise, the meal was quiet and uneventful. Now and then she caught Lisa watching her, her dark eyes lit with an unholy gleam. The first time Danielle met that gaze she felt a small frisson of unease. Lisa was up to something, she thought. But Lisa said nothing untoward, and gradually Danielle relaxed.

After lunch Lisa suggested they go to the pool. Wearing one of her new bikinis, her body well oiled for protection against the afternoon sun, Danielle lay back and closed her eyes.

She jerked when Lisa said, 'That was quite some performance your fiancée put on last night, Sterling.' There was heavy emphasis on the word 'fiancée'. 'She was *so* sexy, wasn't she?'

'I thought so.' Sterling sounded amused.

'How ever did you manage to contain yourself? Poor Sterling, it must have been unbearable for you—' Lisa's tone dripped her usual poison '—Danielle looking like some high-class slut. Weren't you just dying to go to bed with her?'

Danielle's eyes were wide open now. Sterling didn't answer, but she saw him grin.

'Pity your fiancée is so old-fashioned. So frustrating for you. Means you'll never have her in your bed, will you?'

'I wouldn't say that,' Sterling drawled.

'It's obvious. She'll never come to you without marriage—and that's not on the cards. Never really has been, has it?'

'Hasn't it?'

Lisa gave her familiar laugh. 'You're not kids. You've nothing to wait for. If you were really going to get married, you'd have set a date by now.'

'Honey...' Marcus admonished.

Danielle was rigid now. Through her tension she wondered why Lisa was behaving so stupidly. Didn't she care that her husband might be suspicious? Or had the events of the previous night made her so jealous, so angry that she was driven to say things she would later regret?

'Lisa...' Danielle began in warning.

But Lisa ignored both Danielle and Marcus. 'If you were really serious,' she taunted, still looking at Sterling, 'you'd go ahead and set a wedding date.'

'Actually, I was thinking of next weekend,' Sterling said, so calmly that for a moment Danielle wondered if she was dreaming. She stared at him, dazed.

'*Well!*' Just one word from Lisa Renfield. She was pale all at once. The provocative expression had left her eyes, and she had the look of a woman who had embarked on a bluff, only to find it flung right back in her face.

Danielle did not notice her pallor. Her heart was beating so hard that it felt like separate hammer-knocks against her ribs.

'Don't I have a say in this?' she whispered through dry lips.

Sterling smiled at her. 'Sure you do, darling. If next weekend doesn't suit you, we can pick another date instead.'

She could only marvel at his easy smile, at the aplomb with which he had responded to Lisa's provocation. But then he obviously thought that Danielle would know how to take his words: as part of the act played out for the benefit of the Renfields. Obviously, he had not really meant what he'd said.

The other three were all looking at her now: Lisa, tight-lipped and outraged; Marcus, maliciously amused; and Sterling, smiling and relaxed. Danielle was both angry and confused. She was not the one who had started this game, yet they were all waiting for her answer to Sterling's question.

'It's not possible...' she said. 'That is, I can't—' She stopped.

'Why the hesitation, Danielle?' Lisa sneered. She had regained her composure remarkably quickly. 'You're engaged, in love—so you say. You have a ring to prove it.'

'Yes, but—'

'Are you saying you're *not* in love with Sterling?'

'It's not that,' Danielle said painfully.

Sterling helped her out. 'I've taken Danielle by surprise, haven't I, darling? It's true, we hadn't arranged a definite date yet, and she may be wondering how she can get organised so quickly.' He looked at Lisa and Marcus. 'I was going to ask you if we could have the wedding here.'

'Here?' Lisa looked as startled as Danielle felt.

Oh, Sterling was smooth. But he was playing an exceedingly dangerous game now. If he didn't know how to extricate himself from the situation, he could find himself in an embarrassing spot. And wouldn't that serve him right? Danielle thought grimly.

'I was thinking of a wedding on the lawn,' Sterling suggested.

'By all means.' If Marcus was surprised, he did not show it. His manner was as urbane as ever.

Sterling turned to Lisa with a smile. 'Would it be too much to ask you to arrange it? You're so good at arranging parties. Last night was fantastic.'

Lisa directed a look at a visibly distressed Danielle. 'I'll be happy to do it,' she said.

'What on earth are we going to do?'

In her room late that evening, after the last goodnights had been said, Danielle at last had a chance to talk to Sterling. Half a day had passed since his unexpected suggestion. In that time a multitude of arrangements had already been made: Lisa had arranged for a minister, told the gardener to prepare pots of flowers for the area where the ceremony would be held, called caterers and discussed all the requirements for a champagne reception, asked Danielle and Sterling for a list of guests to be invited.

Through it all Danielle had been like a statue, silent and frozen. All her attempts at excuses and delays had been swept aside. She felt as if she was trapped in some dreadful nightmare from which she must surely wake. Yet with every hour that passed the wedding became more of a certainty.

Sterling smiled at her. 'We'll go through with it, of course.'

'You can't mean that!' She stared at him, ashen-faced.

'Why not?'

'It's a sham, that's why.'

'Try telling the Renfields that.'

'Lisa didn't really mean us to get married. You know that, don't you, Sterling? When she challenged you to set a date, she never thought you'd really do it.'

'Why ask the question in that case?'

'She was just punishing me for last night.' Danielle was distraught. 'Punishing me for wearing the black dress. For upstaging her at her own party. For tempting Marcus to flirt with me. She never for a moment thought we'd go through with a wedding. Don't you see, Sterling? Knowing our engagement was only a charade, she was certain we'd take fright the moment a wedding was so much as mentioned. You'd make some transparent excuse and I'd be humiliated. That was what she was after; she wanted to see me squirm.'

'I don't know about you, Danielle, but I don't take fright that easily.'

She looked at him wide-eyed. 'What are you saying?'

'You don't deserve to squirm.'

'Try telling *that* to Lisa.'

'I'm saying it to you, Danielle. You can only be humiliated if we back out of the wedding.'

She was silent for a long moment, wishing she knew what he was thinking, puzzled that he did not see how they had been trapped by Lisa's taunts.

'We have to get out of it; we don't have any other option,' she said at length.

'Sure we do,' Sterling countered easily. 'We'll let Lisa go ahead with the arrangements.'

'We can't do that!' Danielle's voice shook. 'We have to back out, and we can't wait to do it. Not with all the preparations that have already been made.'

'We will not back out.' Sterling's tone had a ring of assurance that had Danielle's head jerking up.

'You can't mean that,' she whispered.

'I've never been more serious.'

'But Sterling...we'd just be extending the charade. The engagement was bad enough. But a wedding! That's real. Final. And there's Toby—' She stopped. 'Besides...'

'Besides what?'

'There's also Lisa. Your relationship with her.' It hurt to say the words.

'Let me worry about Lisa,' Sterling said crisply.

Hope flared. 'Are you saying it's over with her?'

'I'm saying all you need concern yourself with is being a lovely bride.'

The momentary hope died. Suddenly Danielle was very angry. 'This is just one more part of the game to you, isn't it, Sterling? It can't be that for me. Marriage is serious. We can't go through with it; you know we can't.'

'Is the idea of marrying me so terrible?' Sterling's eyes were shuttered, their expression impossible to read.

Danielle looked at him wordlessly. With every passing day she loved him more deeply. There were nights when she ached with the yearning to be with him, when she had to fight the temptation to forget her pride and go to his room and beg him to make love. More than anything, she wanted to spend the rest of her life with him. At the same time, pride and a sense of self-esteem dictated that she could not marry a man who only wanted her for reasons of his own—who would never love her as she loved him.

'Well, Danielle?' he asked softly.

Tears formed in her throat and behind her eyelids. Swallowing hard, she turned her head away from him.

'Is it so terrible?' he persisted.

'You can ask me that?' she asked painfully. 'Yes, we had a holiday romance, but that has nothing to do with what's happening now.' She rubbed angrily at her eyes where the tears were threatening to spill. 'I shouldn't have to spell it out for you. This marriage can't possibly work.'

'It can—if we make the best of it.'

She was desperate now. 'I don't believe that! And we don't have to. There's still time to get out of it.'

'No, Danielle.'

'I won't do it, Sterling.'

'I think you will.' He sounded amazingly sure of himself.

'I don't understand you,' she said slowly. 'This afternoon, when you came out with that outrageous suggestion, I was certain you were only playing Lisa at her own game. I was so sure you'd find a way of backing down.'

'You thought wrong, Danielle.'

'I guess you can't bear to lose face with the Renfields. But you'll have to.' She lifted her head at him. 'I refuse to marry you, Sterling. Not under these circumstances.'

He looked at her for a long moment. There was a tightness in his jaw now and his eyes were hard to read. For no good reason, Danielle found herself suppressing a sudden shiver of apprehension.

'We will be married,' he said finally.

'No.' Her voice shook.

'Wait here,' he told her. 'I've something to show you.'

Tensely, Danielle watched Sterling leave the room. She could not imagine what he wanted to show her. Certainly, there could be nothing that would induce her to change her mind. She would not allow herself to be forced into a meaningless marriage.

Minutes later he was back, carrying a long envelope. 'Take a look at this,' he told her.

She took the envelope from him. With trembling fingers she opened it and drew out two sheets of typed paper. The typed words were a blur as she stared at the signature. *Her own signature.*

'Remember signing this, Danielle?'

'In your office...'

'That's right.'

'The day I agreed to travel with you. Why are you giving it to me now, Sterling?'

'You don't know, Danielle?'

'Of course not. Not that it matters; it doesn't mention a wedding, Sterling. I'd know if it did.'

'Read it, Danielle.' His tone was terse.

It didn't take her long to read the document. She had agreed to travel with Sterling, to take on the duties he assigned to her; she had undertaken not to change her mind and back out of the trip prematurely. Near the end was a clause in which she had agreed to take on whatever additional duties might be asked of her.

When she looked up at him she was ashen. 'Does this mean what I think it means?'

'What do you think, Danielle?'

'You can't force me to marry you!'

'You've read the agreement.'

'You didn't explain it to me, Sterling.' She was shaking.

'You could have asked me to—though it was set out so clearly I'd have thought no explanations were necessary. You're an intelligent woman, Danielle. Didn't you read the agreement before signing it?'

'Yes,' she said tightly, 'but I didn't stop to analyse every clause in detail.'

His eyes gleamed. 'That's always a mistake.'

'I didn't think I had to,' she flared at him. 'I understood the gist of it and that seemed enough. I thought the agreement had to do with secretarial duties. It never occurred to me that you would use this—this outrageous piece of paper to trick me.'

'If you choose to think of it as a trick...' he said softly.

Unnerved, she stared at him. 'You wouldn't really hold me to this, would you, Sterling?'

'Yes, my darling, I would.'

'Don't say that word when you don't mean it,' she snapped.

He smiled at her, and she felt even more unnerved.

'What happens if I refuse to go through with the marriage, Sterling?'

'You lose all the money you would have been paid. You lose your job with the company.'

Once again the little house, the haven she was so close to providing for Toby and herself, appeared momentarily before her eyes. She would lose that too, she realised.

'If I wanted to,' Sterling said quietly, 'I could even sue you for breach of contract.'

The blood left her cheeks. 'You can't mean that!'

He was relentless. 'I didn't say I would—but I could.'

His eyes held hers—watchful eyes, alert and penetrating. She wondered if he could see the welter of emotions struggling within her. After a moment she looked away from him.

'If...*if* I agree to marry you, we both know there'd have to be a time limit.'

When he did not answer, she looked back at him. *'How long, Sterling?'*

Dark eyes met hers. 'As long as it takes,' he said enigmatically.

'Why?' Danielle asked, after a long moment. 'Why do we have to do this?' And then, answering her own question, she added, 'Because of Marcus? Because he might guess the truth? That's it, isn't it, Sterling? You're prepared to go through with a wedding because you don't want to lose the goodwill of the man you've been trying so hard to do business with.'

'That's my Danielle.' Unaccountably, Sterling was laughing. 'Always ready with her conclusions.'

'Am I wrong?'

'I haven't said you're right.'

She looked at him uncertainly, wishing she knew the thoughts behind the sparkling dark eyes. 'There's time,' she pleaded. 'Let's just tell Lisa we've changed our minds.'

'No.'

'But what about afterwards? When we went into this *financial arrangement—*' she emphasised the last two words '—we never imagined anything like this.'

The laughter vanished from Sterling's eyes. 'We'll deal with it,' was all he said.

CHAPTER EIGHT

'WHAT kind of wedding cake would you like, Danielle? Chocolate or plain?'

'Why don't you make the choice, Lisa?'

'You don't prefer one to the other?'

'Chocolate would be nice, but it's not important.'

'Well, I'll think about it. I want everything to be absolutely perfect. I'm so excited about this wedding.'

'Are you really?'

'You don't believe me?'

'No,' Danielle said flatly, 'I don't. I think you were just baiting us yesterday, urging Sterling to set a wedding date, certain he'd find an excuse not to. I saw your face when he suggested the date and I knew you weren't pleased.'

'I am now.' Lisa's dark eyes shone with their usual venom. 'Don't you see, Danielle? This is really great! Sterling and I will be able to get together without fear at last. With Sterling married, Marcus will have no more reason to be suspicious.'

Over the sick feeling engulfing her chest and throat, Danielle said, 'Is that really what you think?'

'Well, sure. Did you imagine Sterling and I would end our relationship once you were married? Good grief, Danielle, I thought I made the situation clear—even you can't be as naïve as all that.'

'Naïve? You didn't think we'd get married at all. I believe when you talked about a wedding you were just bluffing.'

Lisa looked taken aback, but only for a moment. 'Perhaps I was—at that moment. The thing is, Sterling took me up on my bluff. He's smart, and when I thought about it I realised it was perfect. Your marriage will make

137

an ideal front. I say it again—Sterling is one very smart man. It didn't take him long to see the advantages of a wedding.'

'It doesn't occur to you that we could be serious about wanting to spend our lives together?'

Lisa's laughter was hard and scornful. 'Give me a break, Danielle; we've already talked about that. We both know the truth.'

There were things that Danielle would have liked to say to Lisa, but she decided to keep silent. She had fought back once already, with disastrous results. She was not ready for more.

Later that day, Marcus said, 'That's some diamond your fiancé gave you, Danielle.'

She looked down at the ring, brilliant in the sunshine. 'It's very nice.'

' "Nice" isn't the word to describe it. Do you know, I've never had a proper look at it? Let me see it, Danielle.'

Heart sinking, Danielle glanced at Sterling. His eyes were without expression, giving her no assistance.

'I don't think...' she began.

But Marcus was reaching for her hand, and short of pulling away there was little Danielle could do. Tensely, she waited for the put-down that would come when her host had examined the ring and pronounced it a fake.

'Superb,' Marcus declared at last. 'I've seen many fine diamonds in my time, but never one quite like this. Must have cost you a pretty penny, Tenassik.'

Danielle gasped at the incredible figure that Marcus suggested. Without thinking, she darted a look at Sterling. He was waiting for her, his eyes gleaming, lips tilted in the ghost of a grin. On the periphery of her vision she saw Lisa pout.

A little later, when they were alone at last, she was able to ask Sterling about the ring. 'Is Marcus right? Is it really a diamond?'

'You heard what the man said.'

'He implied he was an expert...'

'Then maybe he's right.'

'I was so sure it was a fake.'

Sterling laughed. 'Sorry to disappoint you.'

'Why didn't you tell me?'

'Would it have mattered?'

'I wouldn't have wanted it. I certainly wouldn't have taken it off and left it lying in a drawer; I'd have been petrified. I guess I'll have to wear it all the time now.'

'Would you like it better if it were a fake, Danielle?'

Her answer came swiftly. 'Yes!'

Sterling looked at her quizzically. 'Offhand, I can't think of another woman who'd prefer a fake to a beautiful diamond. Why are you so different, Danielle?'

'Need you ask? You know how I feel about our charade. I'm absolutely sick about it, Sterling, even more so now that we're about to make a mockery of marriage. I have nothing against diamonds; the tiniest chip would be infinitely precious to me if it were given in love—I've told you that before. *Mutual* love, Sterling, *mutual* commitment. That's all that matters to me, not the size or the shape or the cost of a jewel.'

He was looking at her oddly. Suppressing a shiver, she asked, 'Why did you give it to me? Why am I wearing this very expensive ring?'

'Can you think of a reason, Danielle?' he asked softly.

Lisa's words came back to her. 'You owned it already; you were just lending it to me for a short while.'

'Anything else you can think of?'

'You knew Marcus was an expert, that you couldn't fool him with a fake. You knew it had to be the real thing.'

'A costly pretence,' Sterling mocked.

'Not if you'd arranged with the jeweller beforehand to give back the ring when you had no more use for it.' She looked at him questioningly. 'Am I right?'

'Danielle, my darling Danielle.' He was smiling now, his eyes sparkling, his teeth very white against his tan; it was a smile that made her heart turn a little somersault of pleasure. 'Always drawing conclusions. And always wrong.'

'I've asked you not to call me "darling" when you don't mean it,' she said crossly, and he laughed again. 'And about my conclusions—why don't you set me straight if I'm wrong?'

'I'm waiting for you to come up with the right one.'

'If I don't?'

'That would be too bad,' Sterling said.

In the late afternoon she asked Sterling to go for a walk with her. They went through the garden, in the direction of the fields. Shadows were beginning to form along the ground and dusk was not far off.

When they were out of sight of the house, Sterling took her hand. 'What is it, Danielle?'

Turning her head, she looked at him wordlessly. After a moment she said, 'We haven't talked about Toby.'

'Well?' In seconds his expression was hard.

Danielle's voice shook. 'You know by now that he's the joy of my life.'

'Yes.'

'But you haven't said how he would fit into our so-called marriage.' She lifted her head, her eyes darting him a challenge. 'Wherever I go, Toby goes too. The two of us are one package.'

His eyes lingered on her face, disturbing her with the intensity of their gaze. 'You've made that clear already.'

'Knowing that he'd live with us, you're still prepared to go ahead?'

A glimmer of a smile lit the dark eyes. 'Yes.'

'I don't understand, Sterling.'

'Why not, Danielle? I've got to know the child. I like him.'

'That may be true, but I don't believe the prospect of his presence in your life fills you with delight. From the moment you heard I had a son you've been so full of contempt.'

'A contempt that has nothing to do with Toby. It's not his fault if his mother kept two men on a string at the same time.'

At her sides Danielle's hands clenched into painful fists. Her throat felt raw, her lips dry. 'It can't work, Sterling. All his life Toby has known nothing but love. I refuse to marry you if there's going to be a strain. *Even if I lose all the money you were going to pay me.* It wouldn't be fair to my child.'

For a while there was silence. Danielle waited tensely. Then Sterling said, 'I understand that.'

Astonished, she stared at him. 'Why the change of heart?'

'Let's just say I'm prepared to make the best of the situation.'

'A bad one,' she taunted.

Sterling's only answer was a brooding look.

'Talk about having a price tag,' Danielle said bitterly. 'It sickens me when I think of the lengths you'll go to for the sake of business. I believe you'd sell your soul to get what you want. You've never said, Sterling—*how long* will our so-called marriage last? Until the contract with Marcus is signed?'

A glitter appeared in Sterling's eyes. 'My business with Marcus is long-term.'

'Meaning?' Danielle demanded.

'It could last a few years.'

'*Years!* I didn't know that.' Danielle was shaken. At the same time she was also wildly excited.

'That's right.' All at once his expression was odd.

'How many years? *How long, Sterling?*'

'As long as it takes,' he told her insolently.

'You love that phrase; you use it all the time.' Danielle's voice tightened at the sardonic look in

Sterling's eyes. 'Obviously it won't be a real marriage.
We still have to agree on terms and conditions.'

'We did that once before,' he mocked, 'and look where
it got us.'

She stared at him uncertainly, wondering what exactly
he meant. After a moment she said, 'We *must* know
where we stand. How long we need to stay together,
sleeping arrangements—things like that.'

Suddenly he was grinning at her. 'Those things will
take care of themselves.'

'That's not good enough,' Danielle said flatly. 'I need
real answers—don't you understand?'

'No more answers, Danielle.' Still that maddening grin.
'I've told you all I can.'

Danielle stayed awake for hours that night, thinking
about the proposed marriage. Money could never be
enough of an incentive to give in to Sterling's demands,
even if she was to lose her only chance to buy a house.
But there was another reason—she knew that as she
stared out of the window into the dark night.

Pictures were forming behind her eyes: Sterling and
Toby, bending over the little red fire-truck, running
together with the kite, sharing a meal at the restaurant.
Talking and laughing together, getting on well. 'I like
Toby,' Sterling had said more than once.

If Danielle married Sterling, she would be giving Toby
a father—the father who was his. Sham marriage or not,
Toby deserved to have a life with the man who had helped
to bring him into the world.

'Discord in paradise?' Lisa enquired brightly the next
morning.

For once, the four of them were eating breakfast
together. Danielle, who had been picking listlessly at her
food, looked up warily. Her head ached after a night in
which she had had almost no sleep.

'Discord?' Sterling repeated. He sounded surprisingly calm.

'Well, yes. I sense something is wrong.'

'Lisa,' remonstrated her husband, but not with any great conviction—as if, Danielle thought, he was as curious as his wife.

Lisa pressed on. 'The two of you went off yesterday billing and cooing like lovebirds. Sterling returned with a face like a thundercloud—sorry, there are things one can't help noticing—and you came back a little later, Danielle, looking... Well, never mind, you don't want to hear it. And this morning you look anything but a radiant bride.'

'People do have differences sometimes,' Sterling said easily.

'Oh.' An unguarded Lisa looked deflated. 'Does that mean the wedding goes on?'

'Of course,' Sterling said. 'In fact, with time running out, I think it's time my lovely bride-to-be got herself a dress.'

Danielle put down her fork. She felt as if she would choke if she took another bite of scrambled egg.

The next day they drove once more to San Francisco. When Danielle had selected a dress—nothing but the most beautiful, the most delicately made, also the most expensive would suit her prospective husband—they knocked on the door of her parents' house.

'Mommy!' Toby was ecstatic. 'And Uncle Sterling.'

'*Uncle* Sterling?' Danielle flinched.

Sterling smiled at the little boy before looking at Danielle. 'We never discussed it. Uncle Sterling is OK, isn't it?'

Danielle's parents were taken aback when they learned of the wedding plans, but they agreed to drive out to the vineyard, and to bring Toby with them.

When Danielle was alone with her parents, her mother said, 'Does he know about Toby?' And when Danielle shook her head she added, 'Shouldn't you tell him?'

Danielle's lovely eyes were troubled. 'I keep wondering about that. If ever the time is right, I will tell him. But that hasn't happened yet.'

Her father looked out of the window into the garden, where Sterling was throwing a ball to Toby. 'I'd want to know if I had a child, Danielle. Especially if that child was going to live with me.'

'Sterling isn't like you, Dad. In Hawaii he made it clear that he didn't want anything except—' Danielle stopped abruptly. When she went on, her voice was grim. 'It would be different if ours was to be an ordinary marriage. If it was going to be a lifetime commitment I'd have told him about Toby long ago. As it is, our relationship isn't intended to last.'

'How long do you think you'll be together?' asked her mother.

'I've asked the same thing, Mom, and Sterling's answer is always the same—"as long as it takes".'

'Do you know what he means by that?'

Danielle looked down at the brilliant diamond, chosen with such care because it would not do for Marcus Renfield to become suspicious. The wedding band that Sterling had picked out that morning was also beautiful.

'I do know,' she said tonelessly.

'Maybe you're wrong... Maybe it will turn out differently.'

'It isn't possible,' Danielle said.

'If Sterling were to adopt Toby...' Her mother had a wistful look. 'Think what it would mean for Toby to have his father's name.'

Danielle briefly closed her eyes. 'I've agreed to the marriage so that Toby can spend some of his formative years with his father. But it can never be more than that.'

'I'm sorry, I just thought...' Her mother touched her hand. 'I can't help seeing the way you look at him. You've fallen in love with him all over again, haven't you?'

'I never stopped loving him,' Danielle said.

*   *   *

A hush descended over the garden as the bride walked along a red carpet to where her bridegroom was waiting. She looked like a picture, as more than one guest was heard to observe.

Only Danielle's face was not that of a radiant bride; it was a little too pale, the lovely green eyes shadowed. The guests put her pallor down to excitement and a sleepless night. They were right about the latter, though wrong about the reasons.

Standing with his parents, holding a small cushion bearing the wedding ring, was Toby—an excited little boy, his fair hair brushed to a sheen, his blue eyes sparkling, revelling in the attention of the guests.

'*You have a son?*' Lisa had exclaimed incredulously on learning of Toby's existence.

'Yes.' Danielle had been able to grin.

'Then you're not a sex-shy virgin after all. Not the old-fashioned girl you led us to believe you were.' And a moment later she'd said, 'Which confirms what I always knew—you're as sly as they come, and you're only out to get from darling Sterling whatever you can.'

Danielle had not bothered to answer. But she had gained some small shred of satisfaction from seeing the shock in Lisa's face.

The minister began to speak, and as she listened to him Danielle's eyes misted with tears. He talked about a lifetime of sharing and commitment, his words embodying all that she had ever desired. It was brutally ironic that the stuff of her romantic daydreams had turned into this bizarre hoax. For better or for worse, till death us do part—make that for the time Marcus Renfield and Sterling Tenassik do business together, she thought.

It was time to speak their vows. Danielle's voice was low, barely audible. In contrast, Sterling's tone was strong and firm. When he kissed his bride, the embrace was no less convincing. Beside them, Toby gave a little gasp of pleasure.

'You're playing the part to perfection,' Danielle muttered a little later, when she was sure that she would not be overheard.

Her husband of a few hours grinned at her. She had hoped that he would rise to the taunt, but he did not give her that satisfaction.

The wedding ended at last: the congratulations, the kisses, the confetti, the champagne lunch. The last of the guests had left when Danielle went to her room to change. Opening the door of her wardrobe, she gave a little gasp of surprise. Only one outfit was left there— a scarlet trouser suit with a red and white silk blouse.

And then she was looking for Sterling. 'Where are my clothes?' she demanded grimly.

'Packed, if my instructions were followed correctly, and in a case in the trunk of my car.'

'What trick do you have planned for me now, Sterling?'

'Trick?' he drawled.

'What are you doing with my clothes?'

'You'll be needing them where we're going.' There was a wicked gleam in his eyes. 'Some of the time at least.'

She stared at him in dawning comprehension. 'Don't tell me we're going on honeymoon?'

'Newly married couples generally do.'

'*Ordinary* couples. Not you and me, Sterling.'

'You and me too, my darling.'

She let the phony endearment pass; there were more important issues on her mind at this point.

'How about your business with Marcus?'

'The first stage is at an end. We both have some thinking to do now; there'll be more discussions later.'

'Meaning we're free to leave here. That's why my things were packed. You didn't really mean all that silly talk about a honeymoon.'

'Didn't I?'

'You . . . you couldn't have.'

Sterling didn't answer, but his eyes flicked over Danielle's face, lingering deliberately on her lips before moving downwards to her throat, and further still to her breasts and hips and legs. Her heart was suddenly racing.

'You couldn't have meant it, Sterling. Not when we both know that we'll go our separate ways as soon as your business with Marcus is concluded.'

He only grinned at her.

Danielle's heart rate increased rapidly. 'You're not teasing? We really are going on honeymoon?'

'Of course.'

'Where...?' She strove for calm. 'Where are you taking me?'

'To a cabin in the foothills of the Sierras.'

A cabin in the mountains. Alone with Sterling. Time in which to dream, to let herself love him. The thought of it made her feel weak. With an effort she dismissed the lovely picture created by an over-active mind.

'Act two of the play staged for the express benefit of the Renfields,' she said harshly.

'If that's the way you choose to look at it.'

'I could refuse to go.'

'But you wouldn't be so foolish.' He gave a wicked grin. 'Can you imagine what Lisa would say? Would you really give her that satisfaction?'

Danielle bit her lip. 'How long will we be gone?'

'A week.'

'Another week! It's too much, Sterling; I can't do it to my parents. I can't possibly expect them to go on looking after Toby with no help from me.'

'They don't mind.'

'You've spoken to them?' she asked in astonishment.

'Yes. And they seemed quite pleased; they said we should have a good time.'

A fact which her parents, now relaxing in the garden, confirmed. Sterling had succeeded in charming them, Danielle thought grimly. And perhaps they were still hoping that the marriage would last after all. How dis-

appointed they would be when they finally understood
that that would never happen.

Danielle returned to her room and changed out of her
wedding dress.

By the time the bridal couple were ready to leave the
vineyard, Danielle's parents and Toby—hugging a big
teddy bear given to him by Sterling—had already gone.

The Renfields were at the car to say goodbye. Marcus
shook hands with Sterling and kissed Danielle. Lisa
kissed Sterling—very warmly, Danielle noticed. 'Be
seeing you,' she told him, and shot Danielle a telling
look.

A few minutes later they were on the highway. Once
again, Sterling Tenassik, now Danielle's husband—her
husband—had had his way.

The sun was just beginning to set when they came to a
lake. Danielle, who had been expecting a cluster of
dwellings, was taken aback to see just one cabin, made
of cedar logs and A-shaped, situated in lonely splendour
amidst a grove of aspen and spruce trees.

'Our honeymoon hide-away.' Sterling's eyes sparkled
as he smiled at Danielle. 'Bought a few years ago, and
the place I love best in all the world.'

Danielle walked away from him. A wild garden led
from the cabin down to the lake. Rising from the further
shore were the foothills, looming and mysterious, their
gaunt shapes reflected in water turned golden by the
sunset.

She sensed Sterling coming up behind her. 'Like it?'
he asked softly.

'It's absolutely beautiful!'

'I was hoping you'd think so.'

'The most beautiful place I ever saw.'

Sterling's arm went around her shoulders. 'A place
for lovers on their honeymoon?'

'Yes,' Danielle said unsteadily. 'It's perfect for lovers.
But we're not lovers, and this isn't our honeymoon.'

'We were married today.'

'We both know what it was all about. Let's leave, Sterling.'

'No, Danielle.'

'Please! The Renfields needn't know anything about it.'

'No.'

'But there's no reason for us to be here together.'

'None—except to enjoy ourselves.'

Danielle shivered. Sterling's arm was still around her shoulders and the closeness of his body was doing alarming things to her sanity. The temptation to lift her head for his kiss was almost too strong to resist.

'This is crazy,' she said jerkily.

'Well, craziness is for newly-weds . . .'

'But not for us! We both know it. Let's leave, Sterling. Now! Before it gets too dark to see our way on the unlit road.'

'No, Danielle.'

'Please,' she begged. 'We'll find a town, a motel—anything, so long as we can have separate rooms. We can lie low for a while, if that's what you want. Marcus and Lisa won't know where we are; they need never know the truth about our so-called honeymoon.'

'No,' he said firmly.

Danielle was silent for a long moment. At last, the words bumping in her throat, she said, 'I take it the cabin has two bedrooms?'

'Only one.'

'How could you do this to me?'

'We're married,' he said.

'We've been over this! We went through a farce. And now we're stuck—temporarily—in a so-called marriage.'

'Nothing "so-called" about it. Our wedding ceremony was real in every way.'

She looked up at him. His eyes still sparkled. The blood began to race at a frightening pace through her veins.

'You said—' She stopped.

'What did I say?'

'We agreed that this wouldn't be a real marriage.'

'If you think about it, my darling, you'll remember that I never agreed.'

'Don't call me "darling"; you know you don't mean it!' Danielle snapped over a rapidly rising excitement. 'About our marriage, Sterling... We both know we'll be splitting up as soon as we can. Which is why, in the meanwhile...'

'Yes?' A wicked grin appeared on his face.

'No sharing a bed tonight,' she said firmly. 'Or any other night of this sham honeymoon.'

Sterling looked down at her. 'You puzzle me, Danielle,' he said at length.

He was too virile, too ruggedly attractive. His sexiness was raw and throbbing and all-pervading in this lonely place. Danielle found that she had to turn her eyes away from him. 'In what way?' she asked raggedly.

'Four years ago we had a holiday romance. We knew next to nothing about each other, except for the one thing that mattered most—we were wildly attracted to each other.'

'Don't!'

'Sparks flew every time we touched. After the first few days we couldn't spend enough time in each other's arms.'

'I refuse to listen to this,' she said in a strangled voice.

'And on that last night we made love,' he went on inexorably, ignoring her protests.

'Yes,' Danielle whispered painfully.

'At last we have the chance to repeat what we had in Hawaii. We're alone, Danielle; there are no demands on us; we can spend every moment in each other's arms again.'

'No!'

'You wanted it then.'

'Yes... Yes, I did. But... everything's changed. It's all different now.'

'One thing isn't different. I still want to cover every inch of your beautiful body with kisses.'

'I won't listen to this!' she protested wildly.

His free hand went to her chin, turning her face towards him, forcing her to look at him. 'I believe you're as crazy for me as I am for you,' he said softly.

Danielle lowered her lashes, unwilling for Sterling to read the aching hunger and the intensity of her desire in her eyes. It was difficult to speak. 'Even if you were right... it wouldn't work.'

'Why not?' Sterling demanded. 'We weren't married the first time we were together—we are now.'

'That's just it,' Danielle said painfully. 'Four years ago we were impulsive, spontaneous. We did what we did because we wanted to. I admit there were sparks, and we gave in to them. At least we were honest about it. But this... It's all so calculated. The lengths we've gone to just to fool Marcus... Money changing hands... Marriage... *Marriage*, for heaven's sake! I still can't believe we had the nerve to go through with it.'

'Danielle—'

'All of it because you'll stop at nothing to do business with Marcus. And now this honeymoon. It's just more of the same. Even you must see that, Sterling.'

He was silent for a long time. The arm that held her tightened even more. There was a moment when Danielle thought that Sterling was going to kiss her. But the arm loosened and dropped to his side, and she wished she did not feel so bereft.

'I do see,' Sterling said, and reached for Danielle's left hand.

He drew the rings from her fingers—the beautiful engagement ring and the equally lovely wedding band which had joined it earlier in the day. Puzzled, Danielle watched him slip the rings in a pocket.

'That should solve the problem.'

'What are you up to now?' she asked warily.

Unaccountably, Sterling was smiling. 'Removing the obstacle. With the rings gone, we can pretend we were never married. Forget what happened today, Danielle. Forget the minister, the wedding dress, the confetti. The vows we made. Forget the lot.'

'But it happened.'

'Pretend it didn't. You can do that, can't you, Danielle? Pretend we're impulsive and carefree, eager to do whatever we want. Just as we were in Hawaii.'

Danielle's body was consumed with hunger, with a wild yearning. 'This is crazy,' she said.

'Just Danielle and Sterling, enjoying each other without expectations.'

'There are strings now,' she said slowly.

'Not if we pretend they don't exist. For the next few days, while we're here, we'll be the two people we were then.'

'Oh, God, Sterling...' Her throat was so dry that it was an effort to speak.

'And if that's crazy then let's be crazy. Do you think you can do it, Danielle?'

His eyes were deep and dark, the laughter-lines around them crinkling in the way she loved.

A trembling started deep inside her; the core of her femininity was warm and aroused. It did not seem to matter that Sterling had exploited her shamefully; her love for him was as fierce and enduring as ever.

'Can you do it, Danielle?' He was watching her intently now. 'Can you let us enjoy our time together?'

She looked down at her left hand, free of the rings that she had never felt she owned. Suddenly they were back on a golden beach, with the waves crashing around them. And it was, indeed, as if they had returned to that magic time.

'Can you, Danielle?'

'Yes,' she said, almost inaudibly. 'Oh, yes.'

She heard his groan as he gathered her to him, his body hard and vital against hers, his lips in her hair as he murmured, 'My lovely, lovely Danielle.'

The suitcases were forgotten. Arms tightly around each other, they went into the cabin, not a word passing between them as they hurried to the only bedroom. Once there, however, Sterling proceeded with a slowness that drove Danielle to fever pitch.

He undressed her slowly, taking care to kiss every inch of skin as it was exposed. She saw his eyes worshipping her body, and suddenly any lingering shyness vanished and she was undressing him too. Their first kisses were sweet and tender, increasing to a wild and mutual passion. His lips went to her throat and breasts, igniting fire whenever they touched. And she explored his body with her hands, relearning the shape of him, exulting when she heard him give another ragged groan.

The moment came when they could wait no longer. Lying on the double bed, they joined together in an ecstasy that surpassed anything that had happened until that moment. Danielle felt as if she would explode with happiness. This was like that other time, the night that had resulted in Toby, except that this was even more exciting.

Later—much later—they ate by an outdoor fire. And then it was back into the cabin, and again they made love.

Danielle woke next morning to find Sterling, a warm presence beside her in the bed, watching her as he caressed her naked body.

'How long have you been awake?' she asked.

'A while.' His breath ruffled her hair as he spoke. 'I made it my business to wake before you did.'

'Why?' she asked curiously.

'You ran out on me the last time we made love; I couldn't have that happening again.'

She closed her eyes, savouring his closeness, the male smell of him in her nostrils, the roughness of his skin against her smoothness.

'We're going to enjoy this time together, aren't we, Danielle?'

'Oh, yes,' she said softly, happily.

Sterling must have instructed someone to prepare the cabin in advance: there was food and wine in the kitchen, logs in the fireplace, wild flowers in vases everywhere. But whoever had seen to the preparations had vanished discreetly before Sterling and Danielle had appeared.

One wonderful day merged into the next. They would wake early in the morning and go for a run around the turquoise-watered lake. Sometimes they saw wildlife— an elk or a moose and squirrels across their path. When the sun was high in the sky they would swim in the cold lake water, and afterwards Sterling would towel Danielle vigorously until some warmth returned to her limbs. Late afternoons were spent canoeing, and in the evenings they would barbecue steak or fish.

Sitting by the crackling fire, adding new logs to the flames whenever they threatened to die, Danielle and Sterling talked. Sterling told Danielle more about his family, about his dreams and plans. She told him about her own life too. They talked in a way they had not talked four years ago, for now there were no limits, no terms, no constraints.

Except one. There was not a day when Danielle wasn't tempted to tell Sterling the truth about Toby. She would have done so if only she had known how he would react. The fact was that she did not know, and she could not risk spoiling their newly found intimacy—not yet.

Best of all was their lovemaking. The ecstasy was constant; the excitement of mutual fulfilment never waned. They never tired of each other, and every night they reached new heights.

*   *   *

A week after they'd arrived at the lake, Sterling brought out the hated rings. 'Time to put them on again,' he said.

With a sinking feeling Danielle slipped them back on her finger. The magic week—a week out of time—had come to an end.

With the return to reality there was one thing that worried her intensely.

They had lain together one morning, relaxed in the afterglow of their lovemaking. Sterling had made a joke, and Danielle had raised herself on one elbow, laughing as she joked back at him.

Suddenly, the laughter had died in her throat.

'What is it? What's wrong, Danielle?'

She'd hesitated just a moment. 'Nothing.'

'You look as if you've seen a ghost.'

About an inch from Sterling's navel was a mark, half-moon in shape. Danielle had touched it lightly. 'What is this?'

'A birthmark.'

'First time I've noticed it.' She'd forced herself to say the words casually.

'No reason why you should have. It's not remarkable apart from the fact that other Tenassiks also have it.'

Other Tenassiks... Toby had the same mark, in exactly the same place. When he'd been younger, Danielle had tickled it sometimes when she'd dried him after his bath.

'Other people have birthmarks too.' It had been an effort to hide her rising panic.

'Not like this one—the location, the shape. This particular birthmark is peculiar to the Tenassiks.'

'But Sterling—'

'All this boring talk about birthmarks. I can think of something much more satisfying to do with our time. Come here, Danielle.'

As always, his lovemaking had crowded all other thoughts from her mind.

Yet now, as they closed the door of the cabin for the last time and drove away from the lake, Danielle was quiet. For a while she had been able to push the Tenassik birthmark from her mind. It was uppermost in her thoughts now. Nervously, she wondered if she was going to be able to keep the mark a secret from her husband.

CHAPTER NINE

STERLING had brought Danielle and Toby to a house in Sausalito, on the other side of the Golden Gate Bridge from where Danielle had lived most of her life. It was built on various levels against the mountainside, and the patios and most of the windows had spectacular views over the bay.

The house was quite old, with pink-washed exterior walls and lovely wooden floors and wood-framed windows. Apart from a few necessities—a double bed for Danielle and Sterling, a little one for Toby, an oak kitchen table with matching chairs—the house was empty.

Sterling laughed when he saw Danielle's surprise. 'I only bought the place recently. I'm hoping you'll furnish and decorate it.'

Danielle's face clouded. 'I'll be far too busy.'

'Busy?' An odd look had appeared in Sterling's eyes.

'Starting tomorrow, I'll be back at the office.'

'No, you won't.'

She stared at him in confusion. 'Why not?'

'You're not going back there.'

'That's ridiculous. I have a job.'

'Actually you don't,' Sterling said.

'What are you saying? I'm a secretary. *Your own personal secretary.*'

'Not any longer.' His eyes held hers levelly.

'Is this some kind of joke? I don't understand, Sterling; it was what you wanted. Demanded. You *bribed* me into it.'

'That was then,' he said mildly.

Danielle felt cold all at once. The blood drained from her cheeks. 'You're saying I'm *fired*?'

157

'I'm saying that you're no longer employed by the company.'

'Have I done something terrible?' she asked wildly.

'No, it's not that.'

Suddenly she understood; she wondered why it had taken her so long. 'I married the chief executive,' she said dully.

'Right.'

Danielle lifted her chin. 'You can't do this to me, Sterling.'

'I have to; I'm sorry.'

'No, Sterling! This is the end of the twentieth century, for heaven's sake. Do you really think a husband can forbid his wife to work? I don't need your permission.'

'That's right, you don't.'

'Well, then?' she demanded.

'I'd rather you didn't work—but if you do it won't be for my company.'

'You have some nerve, Sterling Tenassik!' Danielle was furious now. 'I've been at that company almost four years. I was there long before you arrived. I like the place, the people; I enjoy what I do. And now you think you can take it all away from me.'

'You didn't expect this?' He was watching her intently.

'Perhaps I'm very stupid, but no, I didn't.'

'Things have changed, Danielle.'

'They have not,' she said heatedly. 'Oh, I know that we're married—technically, at least—but we both know it won't last.'

'You enjoyed our honeymoon.'

She looked at him, and wished she hadn't. Familiarity had not diminished her emotions or her feelings. Sterling had only to be near her for her heartbeats to quicken, for desire to stir in the most sensitive core of her being.

'I did enjoy it...' Her voice shook.

'Well, then?' he asked.

'All the time we were at the lake we were both just pretending.'

'A satisfying pretence.' There was an enigmatic sound in Sterling's tone.

Overwhelmed by a host of intoxicating memories, she found it an effort to speak calmly. 'Pretence all the same.'

'We can go on pretending, Danielle.'

'Until the moment Marcus Renfield agrees to everything you want,' she said bitterly.

'Listen to me, Danielle—'

'No, *you* listen to me, Sterling.' She turned back to him, her green eyes flashing her anger. 'Pretence is for children. You're not a child, and nor am I.'

When he reached for her and drew her against him, she shuddered. 'I've never thought of you as a child, Danielle,' he said softly. 'Only as a woman. A lovely, sexy, desirable woman. The loveliest woman I know.'

'You don't have to say these things,' she whispered. 'You seem to forget that the time for pretending is over. The rings are back on my hand.'

'I'm saying them anyway.' His breath warmed her face.

'I'd rather you didn't.'

'Why not?'

'You know the reason.' She managed—somehow—to push herself out of his arms. 'Whatever there is between us is only for show. Which is why the honeymoon was a mistake.'

'What makes you say that?'

'For a while it made us forget the way things really are. And now you want to go back to confusing the charade with reality.'

There was a flicker of movement in his face. 'That's been your problem all along, hasn't it, Danielle? You've always been confused.'

She gave her head a violent shake. 'Don't taunt me, Sterling! I can't take it. We both know our marriage doesn't mean anything, that it has to end.'

'I wasn't taunting you,' he said. 'Just trying to tell you there's nothing to stop us from continuing to have a good time together. Take off the rings again if it will make it easier.'

Grimly, Danielle looked down at her hand. 'No.'

'We've always given each other pleasure. In Hawaii. At the lake. Now—if you would let us.'

'*Sex!*' She threw the word at him savagely. 'Why don't you just say it as it is? That's all pleasure means to you.'

His face hardened. 'You like to hurt.'

'I prefer to be direct.'

A glitter appeared in the dark eyes. 'I can be direct too. Let me show you just what pleasure means to me.'

'No!' Danielle protested as Sterling reached for her once more. 'Toby—'

'He's exploring the house. Let me kiss you, Danielle; I promise to stop if we hear him come back.'

She swayed towards him as he drew her closer, her head tilting involuntarily in anticipation of his kiss. His lips were touching hers when sanity returned. With an effort she drew back.

'No. We have to talk.'

His arms tightened momentarily, then dropped away from her. 'OK, Danielle, what do you want to talk about?'

'Money,' she said bluntly. 'And don't tell me we keep getting back to the topic. I *need* to work. I need every cent I can earn, and you know why that is. I have a child to support.'

Sterling's face was hard. 'What about Toby's father? The one you never talk about.'

Danielle's legs shook. 'I . . . I don't want to know.'

'You're prepared to raise your child entirely on your own?'

She forced herself to look at him. 'That's the way it is.'

After a long moment Sterling said, 'I once called you a girl with a price tag. I was wrong about that.'

'Yes . . .'

Suddenly a smile warmed his face. 'I can't stop you finding a job—if that's what you really want.'

'I have to; there's no other way. Don't you see?'

'There is a way.' At her obvious confusion the smile deepened. 'I'll support you and Toby for as long as we're together.'

'No, Sterling.'

'I haven't finished. You've earned a rest from the office. How about taking a break—unless you're raring to get back to a desk, of course—and furnishing this place instead?'

'No.'

'You'd be doing me a favour; I hate living in an empty house. Furniture, paint, carpets, drapes. Money's no object. There'll be no deadlines. Take as long as you like.'

The offer was tempting—more tempting than Sterling could ever have guessed—but there were things that Danielle dared not let herself forget.

Somehow she found the strength to shake her head. 'I don't think so.'

'Why not?'

'When our marriage ends—and we both know it has to—you'll marry someone else. Lisa, perhaps...' It was painful to say the last words.

His eyes gleamed. 'Lisa is already married, and not about to leave her husband.'

'Some other woman, then. Whoever she is, she may not want to live in a house that I furnished. She'll have her own ideas.'

'I want *you* to decorate my house, Danielle.' His eyes were warm with devilment.

'Sterling—'

'Please.'

Still she hesitated. 'You might not be happy with my choices.'

'I'll take my chances.'

'You don't know a thing about my taste. You could hate the way the house turns out.'

'Any more excuses, Danielle?'

He was laughing at her. And suddenly she was laughing with him. 'None,' she conceded.

The red-roofed house was the only one that Danielle had ever furnished, and then only in her daydreams, but she set to work eagerly on her new project. Once she had overcome her initial reluctance to impose her ideas on a house which could never be hers, she actually began to enjoy herself.

She went to the fabric and furniture stores of San Francisco and pored over decorating magazines for ideas. She looked at paint swatches and experimented with different colours. In the evenings, when Toby was in bed, she would talk to Sterling about her ideas, about the things she had seen and was thinking of buying.

He asked the same question every time. 'Did you like it?'

'Adored it—but you might not.'

And always there was the sparkle in his eyes. 'If you like it, go for it.'

Danielle took him at his word. She bought furniture and carpets and ordered curtains for every room. Little by little, the house began to take shape. She tried not to think about the fact that it could never be her permanent home.

Life settled into a routine. Despite her defiant words the day they had moved into the house, they lived like a family—Danielle and Sterling and their son. It seemed impossible to do otherwise. They ate together, played together, had fun together. At night, because Danielle could no more resist Sterling's advances than she could stop the breath moving through her lungs, they made love. And their lovemaking was as tender and as passionate as ever.

Only a few things spoiled Danielle's happiness. One was the birthmark of the Tenassiks.

The thought that Sterling could not see Toby naked never left her mind. She made certain that Sterling was never about when the little boy changed his clothes or had his bath. There was an awkward day when Sterling suggested they go swimming and Danielle had to convince her husband and her son that she was not in the mood. Sterling looked at her curiously, almost as if he sensed her tension, but the moment passed. Sterling did not mention swimming again, but Danielle remained constantly on her guard.

When she wasn't worrying about Toby, there was Lisa Renfield. Lisa phoned often.

'Lovely to hear your voice, Danielle.' The woman's husky tones had her clenching her teeth every time. 'Still enjoying family life?'

'Of course.'

'Take my advice: make the most of it while it lasts.' And when Danielle was silent she would go on, 'Hubby there?'

Gripping the receiver tightly, Danielle would say quietly, 'Sterling is out.'

'Get him to call me as soon as he gets in, will you?' A slight pause would ensue. And on a new note Lisa would say, 'If he doesn't call, if you're stupid enough to "forget" my message, it won't matter—I can always reach him at the office.'

An order and a threat. Danielle had no doubt that Lisa meant it when she said that she would contact Sterling at work, and she could not bear the gossip that would cause. And so she would pass on Lisa's messages, and Sterling would phone the woman back. Danielle never heard their conversations; she left the room every time.

One Sunday morning Danielle opened her eyes and knew at once that the weather had changed. She loved to sleep with the curtains open so that she could see the sky beyond the window when she awoke. For days it had been raining, but on this day the sky was blue and cloudless.

'Sun!' she exclaimed as she jumped out of bed and ran to the window.

Seconds later, Sterling was standing behind her. Below them the bay was clear, with not a vestige of fog. Already, so early in the morning, pleasure craft dotted the water.

'Sun,' Danielle said again.

Sterling laughed. 'You sound like a little girl surprised that summer has returned.'

'I hate the rain. Toby will be excited.'

'No more excited than his mother.' Sterling was still laughing as he folded his arms around her. 'Sun or no sun, you're cold.'

Danielle stood quite still, the view beneath her forgotten as she savoured the feel of Sterling's body, long and hard against hers. It did not seem to matter how often they made love; every time he was able to stir her senses anew, to rouse her to heights that she had never imagined.

'Very cold.' His lips were in her hair.

Actually, her blood had warmed considerably in the last few seconds. Deep inside her hunger stirred, making her feel giddy with desire. At times like these it was hard to remember that their marriage had no meaning. There was only her love for him, and the yearning for fulfilment.

'Cold?' she murmured. 'Do you think so?'

'I know so.' She heard the mischief in his voice. 'I also know a way to warm you.'

'And what way would that be?'

'Let me show you.'

So saying, he picked her up and carried her across the room. Her arms were around his neck as he lowered her onto the bed. He was lying down beside her, gathering her to him, when she said, 'Toby... He'll be up any time now.'

'He was asleep when I looked in on him a few minutes ago.'

'You went to his room?'

'I did.'

'You must have planned to make love.'

His lips nuzzled her throat. 'How did you guess?'

She laughed unsteadily. 'You're a bit of a rogue, aren't you, Sterling Tenassik?'

'Am I?' His own laughter was deep and satisfied. 'Well, maybe so.' His mouth brushed hers, lightly and tantalisingly, sending new shivers shuddering through her body.

'I think you are.'

The tip of his tongue followed the path his lips had taken, then went on to brush her throat. 'And I think you're right. To prove it, I'm going to make wild and passionate love to you. And when we've finished we'll start all over again.'

His mouth moved to her breasts, kissing first one then the other. His body was warm against hers, the movements of his arms and legs deliciously sensuous. And all the while Danielle was growing more and more excited.

Suddenly there was a shout from the other side of the door. 'Mommy!'

Danielle froze. 'Toby?' she called back after a moment, thankful that the door was locked.

'Let me in!'

'You said he was asleep,' Danielle whispered to Sterling.

Sterling's voice was low too. 'He was. He must have woken.'

'What are we going to do?'

'Do you want to stop?'

She could not have put an end to their lovemaking. Not at that moment.

'Mommy!' Toby called again.

Danielle raised herself on one elbow. 'Go and play in your room for a while, honey,' she called.

'OK,' Toby said after a second. There was a sound of feet shuffling away from the door.

Danielle and Sterling held each other for a few minutes in silence. Then, very quietly, they began to kiss once more.

For a while afterwards they lay close together, wrapped in the warm afterglow of their lovemaking. Charade their marriage might be, but their pleasure in each other never waned.

When Danielle emerged at length from the bedroom, her lips were tilted in a soft smile and her eyes glowed. It did not seem to matter that Sterling could look at her face and read her emotions, that there were moments when she could hide nothing from him.

In the kitchen she began to make the pancakes that both Sterling and Toby enjoyed. Toby liked to help her, and she called to him. When he did not answer, she went to his room.

In the doorway she stopped. The room was empty.

'Toby?' she called again.

No answer from the child.

Danielle began to look elsewhere. Toby wasn't in the family room, where his toys were kept, or in the den, where he liked to watch TV. She ran from one room to another, but the little boy was nowhere to be found.

'*Sterling!*' she shouted, distraught. And when he came to her she cried, 'It's Toby; he's disappeared!'

'You're trembling. Calm down, darling; he has to be in the house.'

In her panic, she did not register the endearment. 'I've looked everywhere.'

'Danielle—'

But she was already running to the front door, Sterling at her side. The door was locked, as they had left it the previous night. They raced to the back door. It was slightly ajar, a breath of cool morning air coming in from outside.

'He's left the house!' Danielle exclaimed.

Sterling tried to reassure her. 'He's a good kid; he won't have gone far.'

'You're right, I know.' But she could not shake off her fear.

They went out to the street and she called, 'Toby! Toby, where are you?'

Still no answer.

At a crossroads near the house they hesitated, wondering which way to proceed. A man walking his dog said he had seen a little boy running off to the left. A moment later Danielle and Sterling were going that way, calling Toby's name as they went.

Danielle's heart was beating hard and her throat was dry with fear. She blamed herself for Toby's disappearance. If only she and Sterling had stopped their lovemaking the moment the child had called. If only she hadn't told him to go and play. If only...

She gasped with pain when her foot turned on a stone concealed beneath a clump of leaves. A second later she was sliding to the ground.

Stopping in his tracks, Sterling reached down a hand. 'Are you OK?'

'Yes!'

He helped her up, but when she tried to stand the pain caused her leg to crumple and she sank back to the ground.

Sterling crouched beside her, but she waved him away. 'Keep going; you have to find Toby. *Please!*'

'Right.'

She clung to him tightly for a moment. 'I'm so frightened.'

'I'll find him for you,' Sterling promised.

Ten minutes later he was back, dark eyes sparkling. He held a dishevelled, pyjama-clad child by the hand.

'*Toby!*' Danielle was weak with relief. 'Where on earth did you go?'

'Up the street,' the child said.

'Why didn't you stay in the house?'

'I saw a puppy. It was lost, but a man found it.'

'Toby decided to go after the pup. It's the kind of thing boys do.' Sterling grinned down at her, and she heard the unspoken message in his tone: Toby's a boy; you can't coddle him for ever. Don't make too big a deal of what he did.

Danielle understood. But she had to say the words nevertheless. 'You had quite an adventure, honey, but don't run off again. Wait for me next time and I'll come with you.'

'Come see the puppy,' an unrepentant Toby shouted.

'I think we should get your mom up off the ground,' Sterling said, and reached for Danielle.

Once more, unsuccessfully, she tried to stand. A moment later Sterling had scooped her up into his arms and was carrying her easily along the street and into the house.

Despite all her protests, he insisted on taking her to a doctor. As Danielle had suspected, she had sprained her ankle. An hour later, her ankle bandaged, they were back at the house. Sterling carried her inside, put her gently down on the bed, and brought her a cup of hot tea— all with a tenderness that made her feel weak.

The doctor had given her a shot to relieve the pain. It made her so drowsy that she was soon asleep.

Later—much later—she opened her eyes. A light was on in the room, and behind the windows it was dark. Sterling was writing at a desk on the far side of the room. Danielle called his name.

He spun around. 'You're awake,' he said abruptly, the words sounding like an accusation.

Danielle was bewildered and dazed. 'How long did I sleep?'

'Most of the day.'

'Good grief! Where is Toby?'

'In bed.'

'You took care of him?'

'I did.'

Sterling left the desk and strode across the room. He stood beside the bed. His expression was dark and dangerous.

Danielle was suddenly tense. 'Sterling—what's wrong?'

'You can ask me that?' His neck was corded, his shoulders rigid. 'Why didn't you tell me about Toby?'

'Toby...' Deep inside Danielle a great trembling began.

'He's my son.'

Danielle stared up at Sterling. His face was an icy mask.

'He is my son, isn't he?' he demanded.

Danielle could only look at him wordlessly.

'Damn it, Danielle, *answer me*! Toby *is* my son, isn't he?'

Her throat was so tight that it was difficult to get out the one word. 'Yes.'

'I knew it!'

'The birthmark,' she whispered.

'The Tenassik half-moon, just next to his navel. Identical to mine. I remember we talked about it.'

'Yes...'

'I helped Toby with his bath. Can you imagine how I felt when I saw the mark?' Beneath his tan Sterling was pale and his eyes were dark pools.

'Sterling—'

'In a second my world changed. Nothing was as I'd believed it to be. Toby saw my shock and I had to cover up, pretend nothing had happened.'

'Sterling—' she tried again.

'And all the while I could think of only two things: I am a father, and the woman I thought I was in—' He stopped abruptly. When he went on his voice was cold.

'Toby's mother, the woman I married, didn't have the decency to tell me I had a son.'

He towered above her, a threatening figure of a man. 'Why, Danielle?'

Danielle was trembling quite violently now. She did not know what to say. Sterling had taken her by surprise; she needed time to think about her answer.

As she stared at him, his expression become more threatening still. 'Don't look at me with those big green eyes,' he warned roughly. 'Eyes a man could lose himself in if he allowed himself to. I know—it almost happened to me.'

'What are you saying?' Danielle asked unsteadily.

'It doesn't matter,' Sterling answered her grimly. 'Not now. Not any more. There was a time when I thought that you and I could—'

'Could what?' She was a little breathless.

'I just told you, it doesn't matter.'

'Sterling—'

'There's only one thing I want from you now: answers.'

Tears were beginning to clog Danielle's throat, but she swallowed hard. 'You already know Toby is your son.'

'I have to know how you could have the nerve to keep the truth from me. The day you told me about Toby, I wondered if he was my child—you knew I was curious—but from the way you spoke I gathered he must have been conceived after we were together.'

Her trembling increased.

'How could you do it to me, Danielle?'

'I was going to tell you.'

'Hard to believe.'

'I was waiting for the right time.'

'You had every opportunity.'

'No,' she said slowly, 'I did not.'

'What were you waiting for?'

A hint that there was something other than a strong sexual attraction in their relationship, she thought. A suggestion that Sterling regretted the agreement they had made in Hawaii. That their time together had been more than just a brief holiday romance.

'I can't tell you that,' she said tonelessly.

'I see.'

'I'm sure you don't.'

He looked at her in contempt. 'That's where you're wrong, Danielle. I see a lot more than you realise. I see a woman with the face of an angel, who lives by deception and lies. A woman who made quite certain that her child's father would never see him undressed. Do you think I don't understand now why we could never go swimming, why I was never allowed to be present when Toby had his bath? For reasons of her own, that woman—my wife—had no intention of letting her husband know that he had a child.'

A little desperately, Danielle said, 'Why ask questions when you think you have all the answers?'

'Answers that fill me with disgust. I had the *right* to know I'd fathered a child. *An absolute right, Danielle.* You believe Lisa is a woman without morals. Sure, she cheats on her husband, and, contrary to what you've always thought, I don't happen to think what she does is right. But you're without morals too, Danielle. And your sins are much worse than Lisa's. There's no way you can justify them.'

There were things that Danielle wanted to say, but Sterling was already moving away from the bed. He was at the door when she called him back.

'What happens now?'

'I have no idea,' he said.

She heard him striding down the hallway. The front door slammed. Minutes later Danielle heard his car zipping down the street.

CHAPTER TEN

THE hours passed. In that time Danielle lay in bed, in too much pain to get up. After Sterling's precipitate departure from the house, she had wept. But there were no tears left in her now. Dry-eyed, head throbbing, she stared through the open-curtained windows into the night.

It was almost midnight when Sterling returned. Danielle had not heard his car; she had no idea that he was in the house until he appeared in the doorway.

In a moment she was rigid. 'You're back.'

There was not a flicker of expression in the rugged, hard-boned face. 'You didn't think I would come?'

'I didn't know what to think. But I'm glad you're here. We have to talk.'

'It's late,' he said abruptly.

'It won't take long; there's something I need to tell you.'

'Well?'

'Toby and I will be leaving first thing tomorrow.'

'You can't even walk.'

'I'll get my parents to pick us up, so my foot won't be too much of a problem.'

'No,' Sterling said.

Danielle stared at him in astonishment. 'I'd have thought you'd be glad. I'm leaving you of my own free will; I'm sparing you the unpleasantness of having to throw me out.'

'You're going nowhere.'

'Why not? It's obvious that after what happened today you can't stand the sight of me.'

'You're my wife.'

'In name only.'

Sterling's lips tightened. 'My wife all the same.'

Danielle swallowed. 'That's true—in a way.'

His eyebrows lifted; beneath them his eyes were dark and brooding. 'What do you mean, "in a way"?'

She forced herself to meet the autocratic gaze. 'As if you need an explanation! Lisa taunted you about setting a wedding date and you decided to call her bluff. I was being paid to act a part, and I was in a trap.'

'You like to twist the knife, Danielle.'

She looked at him squarely. 'It's clear we can't go on living together. Until we're divorced, we can quite easily live apart.'

'No.'

'I'm sure you'll find a way to make Marcus and Lisa understand.'

'This has nothing to do with the Renfields.'

'What, then?'

'Toby.'

Danielle's head jerked on the pillow. She looked at Sterling, but his expression was impossible to read. Disbelievingly she said, 'That's ridiculous!'

Sterling met her gaze levelly. 'Do you think so?'

'Yes!' Danielle felt an icy shiver of fear run through her. 'Toby means nothing to you.'

'He's my son.'

'You didn't know that until today. I understand your shock, Sterling, but you can't possibly love Toby as I do. He's my life; he's everything that makes living worthwhile. You can see him as often as you want to, but there's no way I'll let him go.'

'Who said anything about letting him go?' Sterling was impatient. 'Toby has a mother and a father and he's going to live with them both.'

The shiver intensified. 'You're not making any sense.'

'No?' He looked down at her, his face rugged and aloof and so devastatingly attractive. 'Do you want to know where I've been, Danielle? I drove up into the hills. I sat in my car, looking down over the lights of the city. I stayed up there for hours, and I did some thinking.'

'You're trying to tell me something.'

'We've talked a fair bit, you and I, since we've come together again. We've told each other things we didn't talk about four years ago. But there's one thing I haven't told you.'

Danielle watched him go to the window. His neck and shoulders were more relaxed than they had been earlier, as if the man who had been so angry with her then had arrived at a decision of some kind. If only she could relax, Danielle thought. Feeling tenser by the moment, she waited for him to continue.

Sterling turned from the window at length and came back to the bed, his expression one of determination.

'My father died when I was quite young,' he said.

'I already know that.'

'What you don't know are the circumstances—I seldom talk about them. Dad died in a boating accident. There was a weather warning the day it happened; my mother pleaded with him not to go out, but he was a fearless sailor and he went anyway. I still remember the shock, the utter devastation when we learned he had drowned. Such an unnecessary death. My mother did an excellent job of raising us—my brother, my sister and me. She worked very hard, made sure we were educated and independent.'

He fell silent. Danielle hid her growing tension. Sterling would speak again when he was ready to.

'There were things my mother didn't have time for,' he said at last. 'Things we missed.'

'Don't you dare drag up stereotypes! In this day and age!' Danielle was outraged. 'Children don't have to have two parents. It's nice if they can have them but it isn't absolutely necessary. A single mother can give her child a good life filled with love and caring. I should know. I've been doing it for quite a while now, and I'm not alone—millions of other women do the same.'

'I'm not denying it; my own mother was one of those women. Thing is, Danielle, Toby has a father who *wants* to be part of his life.'

'We've managed perfectly well until now,' she said wildly. 'We don't need your help, Sterling.'

There was a sudden movement in the hard jawline. Quietly he said, 'Maybe not. All the same, I want to be there for my son.'

Danielle closed her eyes for a few seconds as she tried to make sense of all that had been said. Opening them once more, she looked into the face of the man she loved more than life itself—though he would never know that.

'Are you telling me,' she asked at last, 'that you want our marriage to continue?'

'Exactly.'

'Even though you have nothing but contempt for me?'

'Even so,' he said flatly.

'It won't work, Sterling. It can't.'

'We'll make it work,' he told her, his tone defying any further argument.

After the first raw emotions had faded somewhat, work it did. Miraculously, so it seemed.

When she watched Sterling with Toby—throwing him a ball, teaching the child to ride a three-wheeler, telling him stories—it sometimes seemed to Danielle as if he was actually glad that the little boy was his son. As for Toby, it was clear that he had taken Sterling to his heart, that he accepted him as a family member in almost the same way as he did his mother and his grandparents.

Sterling's attitude towards Danielle was less happy. She would look up sometimes and find him watching her, his eyes narrowed, his lips tight.

'You don't trust me,' she burst out once.

An eyebrow lifted. 'Have you given me cause to?'

She bit her lip. 'You've no right to judge me.'

A harsh laugh greeted the statement. 'You're a strange one to be talking of rights,' he said.

But the weeks passed, and to Danielle's relief Sterling's coldness gradually vanished. Their lovemaking, which had stopped after he learned the truth about Toby, resumed, becoming as passionate as ever. There were days when Danielle actually forgot that her marriage was a farce.

One irritant remained constant, however. Lisa's phone calls to Sterling didn't stop. The woman had no qualms about calling him often, sometimes late at night. Danielle never asked him what they talked about. There was a part of her that was infinitely curious, another part that did not want to know.

One morning Danielle realised that there were certain symptoms which she could no longer ignore. Sterling had already left for work when she went to the telephone.

A few days later, after taking Toby to his playschool, she drove across the Golden Gate Bridge. She did not have to wait very long in the doctor's office, which was just as well, for at this point she was almost bursting with suspense.

The doctor—a woman who had attended to her in the past—examined her thoroughly and then did a test. Not long afterwards Danielle heard the news.

'You're pregnant, Mrs Tenassik.'

'Pregnant!' She felt weak.

The doctor looked at her curiously. 'You suspected it, didn't you?'

'Yes.'

The doctor eyed her with a look of professional concern. 'Anything wrong, Mrs Tenassik?'

Danielle hesitated. 'Not exactly.'

'Is there something you'd like to talk about?'

'No, I don't think so.'

'Forgive me, but I get the feeling you're not happy about this baby.'

'I will be.' For the first time Danielle managed a smile. 'Just as soon as I get over the shock. How far along am I?'

'Six weeks.'

When she left the doctor's office, Danielle was in no mood to go home. Her parents were picking up Toby from his playschool later in the day and she had a few hours to herself. Time to wander a while before making her way back across the bridge.

Around noon she walked into a restaurant on the Embarcadero, where she ordered coffee and a salad. Usually she liked to sit near the window, but today the place was particularly crowded and she had to content herself with a table in the middle of the restaurant.

A baby... Her thoughts turned inwards as she remembered a particular night of impulsive lovemaking and abandoned passion. Normally, they were careful, but that time Sterling had had no protection—shades of their night together in Hawaii. Crazily in love and yearning only for fulfilment, Danielle had coaxed him into making love to her all the same. Afterwards, as they'd kissed and caressed, the last thing on their minds had been another pregnancy.

Lost in her reverie, she paid no attention to the people around her. It was only the sound of a familiar husky laugh that jerked her to reality.

At a table not far from hers were Sterling and Lisa. Deep in conversation, they clearly had not noticed her. Sterling had his back to Danielle, but she could see Lisa's face—the enticing, come-hither smile, the pouting lips.

Danielle watched transfixed as Lisa put her hand over Sterling's. And then they were leaning across the table towards each other. Pain tore through Danielle as she saw them kiss.

A second later she was on her feet. She was at the door of the restaurant when a hand touched her arm and someone said, 'Just a moment, madam.'

She turned and looked into the face of her waiter. Friendliness itself when he had taken her order, his expression was anything but friendly now.

'Your bill, madam,' he said sternly.

The bill! In her shock, Danielle had given no thought to anything so mundane as paying for her food.

'I didn't think... I didn't realise... I'm so very sorry...' Cheeks scarlet with embarrassment, she trembled as she fumbled with the clasp of her purse.

'I'll see to this.' It was a voice Danielle recognised. Sterling was quietly taking charge of an uncomfortable situation.

'I'm sorry, sir; this is between the lady and the restaurant.' The manager had also arrived on the scene by now, his manner as stern as the waiter's. 'I'd appreciate it if you would return to your table.'

'Sterling you don't have to—' Danielle's voice was choked.

Sterling ignored her. 'The bill, please.' Once more he was addressing the waiter.

'You don't understand, sir; the lady didn't pay for her order and we—'

'I understand perfectly.' Sterling's tone was cool, crisp and authoritative. 'The lady wasn't thinking when she got up to leave; there was no intention on her part to defraud you. I insist that you give me the bill. Now.'

Faces at nearby tables were keenly interested. One face was clearer than the rest: Lisa, eyes bright, a malicious smile tilting her lips, clearly enjoying every moment of Danielle's predicament.

The manager and the waiter looked at each other. 'Give the gentleman the bill, Thomas,' the manager said after what seemed like a very long moment, and then he walked away from the scene.

When the bill had changed hands, Danielle was left alone with Sterling. 'I'm sorry; it shouldn't have happened.' Her voice shook.

Sterling's eyes went momentarily to Lisa, then back to his wife. Quietly he said, 'We'll talk about it at home.'

Danielle did not answer him. Without a backward glance she hurried out of the restaurant. Her mind was a turmoil of unhappiness and despair, her eyes were blurred with unwanted tears.

When Sterling walked into the family room a few hours later and said, 'Where is Toby?' Danielle put down the sweater she was mending.

'With my parents,' she said.

'He doesn't usually stay out so late.'

'I called my mother and asked her to keep him there longer.'

'Did you have a reason?'

'We have to talk. Alone.'

'We do indeed,' Sterling said.

And that was no more than Danielle had anticipated. After what had happened in the restaurant, her beloved husband would have a lot to say to her.

'I'll talk first, Sterling.' A firm tone hid her uncertainty.

His gaze swept over her, lingering on stormy eyes and on lips that quivered. In his own eyes was an expression which Danielle had trouble reading.

'Go ahead,' he said.

Now that the moment had come, Danielle's mouth was dry. She knew the risk she was taking, and for one crazy moment she was tempted to change her mind. But that would have been the easy way out.

'About what happened today,' she began abruptly.

Unexpectedly, he grinned. 'Quite an experience.'

Her nails bit hard into the soft skin of her hands. 'You may be able to joke about it. I can't; it was one of the most humiliating moments of my life.'

Sterling laughed softly. 'That's hardly surprising.'

'Can you guess why it happened?'

The laughter vanished from Sterling's eyes. 'I told you I wanted to talk to you about it.'

'And I said I would go first. How do you think I felt when I saw you and Lisa together?'

'Why don't you tell me, Danielle?' he asked quietly, his voice odd.

'Furious. Degraded. Cheap and used.'

'Really?' His eyes were watchful.

'More than anything, I felt exploited. I *hate* the game we've been playing.'

'It's not the first time you've told me that, Danielle.'

'But I've never done anything about it.'

'Are you about to do something now?'

'You bet I am!' She threw the words at him.

'Well?' Sterling said after a long moment.

'I've had all I can take! Do you understand?' Green eyes sparked furious fire at him. 'Lisa's constant phone calls. Her taunts and insults. Your little trysts.'

'Which trysts are you referring to?' Sterling asked.

'After this afternoon you have the nerve to ask me that?'

'What you saw wasn't a tryst,' he said levelly.

'It had every sign of one. The two of you at that table, eyes only on each other, holding hands, kissing. Kissing, for heaven's sake, in the middle of a crowded restaurant! I felt sick when I saw it!'

'And so you ran out without paying.'

Danielle hesitated a moment. 'Yes.'

'You didn't like seeing us together?'

'Us'... The intimacy of the word hurt. 'I hated it,' she said.

'I told you we had to talk.'

Here it was—the little speech telling her that he was in love with Lisa, that he had to be free to go on seeing her whenever he wanted.

But there were things that Danielle had to get in first.

'You can talk when I've finished,' she insisted. 'There's something you have to know, Sterling—I'm no longer prepared to go on with the charade.'

His face was pale suddenly. 'What are you saying?'

'I've done a lot of thinking. About Toby and our marriage. About all that's happened.' She paused a moment. 'I...I came to the conclusion that the only thing that made sense was to leave.'

'Danielle—'

'*No*, Sterling, you have to let me finish!' She took a breath. 'I was going to pack our cases and be out of this house before you got back from work. And then...I thought again—'

She stopped. She was getting to the hard part now.

'Go on,' Sterling said tautly.

'I remembered what you told me about your childhood. About your father. And I...I thought our children should have the things that you missed.'

Sterling was staring at her, his eyes seeming to penetrate to the very centre of her being. 'Did you say *children*?'

'Yes,' Danielle whispered.

She flinched when he seized her shoulders in his large hands. 'Why?' he demanded. 'You could have said Toby.'

Danielle tried to move away from him, but he was holding her too tightly. Her heart was beginning to race, her throat ached with emotion and nerves.

'It...it's not just Toby any more,' she said unsteadily.

'Danielle!' he exploded roughly.

'There's another baby on the way.'

'Why didn't you tell me?'

'Because I didn't know until today.'

She took a shuddering breath. And then she told him about her visit to the doctor and the pregnancy test.

'I didn't know,' she said on a sob.

'My God, Danielle! My darling, are you all right?'

Darling... If only he meant it. 'I'm fine,' she said.

'That appalling experience in the restaurant—you should never have been put through it. I hope it didn't upset you too much. Why didn't you say something? You should be in bed.'

'No,' she said, but Sterling did not seem to hear her.

Ignoring her protests, he picked her up in his arms, carried her to the bedroom and put her, very tenderly, down on the bed.

'Stay there,' he ordered when she tried to sit up.

'But we have to finish our talk.'

'You've said everything that has to be said. Toby is our child. We're having another baby. I won't let you leave. We'll stay together, Danielle. That's all there is to it.'

'No,' she said faintly.

He looked puzzled. 'I don't understand.'

'If I stay—*if*—it can't be only for the sake of the children.'

'There's something else?' Sterling was all intense watchfulness now.

Danielle closed her eyes briefly. This was the hardest part of all.

'The only thing that counts,' she said at length.

'Say it, Danielle!'

She drew breath, then looked at him bravely. 'I'm in love with you, Sterling.'

'Danielle!'

She wasn't certain whether the emotion she heard in his voice was joy, though amazingly it sounded like it. All she knew was that, having gone this far, she had to continue.

'If we stay married, Lisa has to go. For too long I was prepared to put up with the situation. I had to—I was being paid, after all. But not any more, Sterling. I'm sick and tired of Lisa's constant calls. I won't have a husband who cheats on me with another woman. That's what you have to understand. If I remain in this marriage you will have to make a complete break with Lisa.' She hesitated, then said, 'That may not be what you want. Probably it isn't. If...if that's so, I'll pack tonight and go.'

'You're going nowhere, my darling.'

'What...what about my terms?'

'Danielle, my darling Danielle.' He gave a ragged laugh as he drew her against him.

For a long moment he held her in his arms, then he put her gently back against the pillow.

'I told you I had things to say to you too. Are you ready to listen to me now?'

'Yes,' she whispered.

'What you saw in that restaurant wasn't a tryst,' he told her.

'It looked like one.'

'I know, but it wasn't. Lisa's calls were annoying me too. I knew it was time to put an end to them. I asked

her to meet me today because there were things I needed
to tell her.'

'What things?' Danielle asked, a little breathlessly.

'Apart from the fact that there could never be anything between us?' Sterling cupped Danielle's head in
his hands, his thumbs beneath her chin, his fingers
threading through her hair. 'I told Lisa that I was deeply
in love with my wife. That there could never be anyone
else in the world for me except my precious Danielle.'

Danielle thought that she would explode with joy. 'You
didn't!'

'I did, my darling. And, whatever you may think about
Lisa, she understood. Yes, she put her hand over mine,
and yes, we kissed—but it was a farewell kiss. Lisa had
just agreed that she would not get in touch with me again.
What's more, she wished me happiness with my wife.'

'I don't know what to say,' Danielle whispered.

'There is one thing.' Sterling's eyes sparkled. 'Did you
really mean what you said about loving me?'

'Oh, yes!'

'I have to know—when did it happen?'

'On holiday, all those years ago.'

Sterling was quiet for a long moment. When he spoke
again, his voice was rough. 'If that's true—and I find
it hard to believe—why did you run out on me after we
made love?'

'I had to. You'd made it clear you didn't want a permanent relationship.'

He sat upright on the bed. 'You said it first.'

'Yes... No last names, no involvement. I'd been
through something unpleasant; I didn't think I was ready
for anyone else.' She looked at him. 'But Sterling, you
were just as keen to keep things detached.'

'Only because I felt I had to play along with you.'

'*What?*'

'You were so adamant, Danielle. I sensed that you'd
scuttle away at the slightest hint of pressure. Thing was,
from the moment I saw you I was certain I had to get
to know you better. I knew then and there that you were

the only woman for me—always. I also realised that I had to agree to your terms. More than that, it seemed to me that if I pretended to be as keen as you on keeping things light then our romance would have more of a chance.'

'If only I'd known!'

'It wasn't easy for me to go slowly, my darling. I remember wishing I could make love to you right after our first date. It was agony to end the evening with a friendly kiss.'

Danielle gave a ragged laugh. 'I remember that kiss.'

'Our relationship progressed, but I knew I had to let you set the pace. There were nights when I was more frustrated than you can guess, but I couldn't let you know it.'

'We did progress,' Danielle said softly.

'We certainly did. All was fine until we made love. That night, lying with you in my bed, I knew I couldn't wait any longer. The holiday was about to end, I was in love with you—madly in love, Danielle—and I couldn't let you go. I was going to propose to you in the morning.'

Speechless now, Danielle stared at him.

'Imagine how I felt when I woke up and found the bed empty. I couldn't believe it! I rushed over to your hotel. I had to talk to you, propose to you, convince you to marry me. But you were gone. And the concierge refused to give me any information. Name, address—he could tell me nothing at all. I tried bribing him, but he wouldn't budge.'

'What did you do?'

'I ran out of the hotel like a wild man. I was in despair. I had no idea what I'd done wrong, why you'd left me without saying goodbye. I thought I must have offended you in some way; I didn't know how.'

'You didn't offend me, Sterling.'

'Then why? Why did you leave without a word? *I have to know.*'

Danielle took one of Sterling's hands and let her fingers thread through his. It was easy to touch him now without waiting for him to make the first move.

'I was desperate too,' she told him. 'I was a virgin the night we made love. Did you guess? I thought you meant it when you said no strings attached. I believed the last thing you wanted was a permanent relationship. I was sure that if you realised how I felt about you you'd be horrified. I'd fallen in love with you, Sterling, and I was scared that in some unguarded moment I'd find myself asking you for more than you'd want to give.'

'But no goodbye? To leave just like that?'

'I didn't know if I'd be able to say the words without breaking down. I couldn't let you see me cry; I thought you'd hate that. And so I left, very quietly, before you were awake.'

'And told the concierge not give me any information.'

'Yes.'

'What a mess!' Sterling groaned. 'Two people who couldn't communicate honestly with each other.' He was quiet for a long moment. Then he said, 'What happened when you found out you were pregnant?'

'I was so tempted to find you. I didn't know your last name, but I considered hiring a private detective. Yet the more I thought about it, the more I knew I couldn't do it. If you hadn't wanted anything more than a holiday romance, you certainly wouldn't want a child disturbing your life.'

'And afterwards...when we met again...why didn't you tell me?'

'At first you were so cold, so distant that there was no way I could say anything. And later, after we were married... I thought of telling you then, but I felt I couldn't breathe a word while our marriage was only a sham.'

'Our timing was never right, was it?' Sterling said.

'No...'

'Which was why I had to resort to drastic measures.'

Danielle was intrigued. 'What do you mean?'

'A moment ago you said I was cold and distant when we met again. Can you imagine how I felt, Danielle, that day when you walked into my office? Four years of thinking about you, wondering what had happened to you, worrying that you might be married to someone else, and there you were, Miss Danielle Payne, come to take some memos. All that time, not knowing your last name, only to be introduced by an office manager.'

'You shook my hand and acted as if we'd never met. I didn't know what to make of it.'

'Do you wonder? I was shocked, Danielle. Angry too. Don't forget you'd left me on what was supposed to be the most important day of our lives.'

'I think I understand. Now. I didn't then.'

'By the time I'd had a chance to cool down, you were about to hand in your notice. No matter how angry I was, I knew that my feelings for you hadn't changed. I couldn't let you leave the company; I might never have found you again.'

Things were beginning to fall into place. 'And so you lured me into going away with you.'

'That's right.'

'You were so contemptuous when I accepted. You thought I was a girl who would do anything for a price.'

'I'm ashamed of that now. But remember, my darling, I didn't know why you'd left me; I had no idea why you were prepared to go with me once you knew how much I was prepared to pay.'

'Dad wasn't well; I *had* to find a place where Toby and I could make our own home.'

'I know that now. In fact, I realised very quickly that I was wrong. That a diamond meant so little to you. I tried to buy you the most beautiful ring I could find— I didn't know that a piece of glass would have been enough if it was given in love.'

'Yes. Sterling, I don't understand—why did you involve the Renfields? Did you and Lisa—?' She swallowed; even now it was hard to say the words. 'Did you and Lisa have a relationship?'

'We had been friends.'

'More than friends?'

'In a way. Some time ago. Never very seriously, and before Marcus came on the scene. Lisa can be good fun, but I was never in love with her—how could I be when I'd never stopped loving you? Not that Lisa would have wanted me permanently either. Only the richest man she could find would do for her.'

'Why was she in your office that first day?'

'To wish me luck. To flirt a little. To have lunch. As you know, Lisa's not the faithful kind; she needs constant attention from men.'

'Doesn't Marcus mind?'

'Not particularly. He accepts her the way she is; he enjoys having a beautiful young wife and he knows it's unlikely she'll ever leave him.'

'But Lisa hated seeing me with you. She was so certain our engagement was a sham. I could have sworn she was really jealous of me.'

Sterling laughed. 'You still don't understand, do you? Lisa has been through a lot of men in her life. She discards them without mercy, but it pleases her to believe that she retains her hold over each one of them. That's why she continued to call me, to see me. It didn't mean anything to either of us—it never did—but she went on with it all the same. I had a feeling she would react just the way she did when I brought you to her home.'

'I still don't know why you did that.'

'I was hoping you'd feel just a little bit jealous too, my darling. I thought Lisa might goad you into doing things you might not do otherwise.'

'Like wearing the black dress,' Danielle said ruefully.

'Wasn't that something?' Sterling's eyes were warm with mischief.

'And agreeing to marry you.'

'Precisely.'

'But Sterling, you only suggested the wedding date after Lisa taunted us.'

Sterling laughed. 'I didn't need Lisa's taunt. True, I seized the moment to set the date, but I had intended doing so anyway a day or two later. My plans were laid all the time.'

'Including getting me to sign that vile piece of paper.'

'Was it vile?' He laughed again, then answered his own question. 'Yes, my darling I guess it was. It was outrageous—I knew that at the time. Thing is, I thought that if I proposed you might turn me down. I needed an iron-clad way of getting you to marry me.'

'It's not nice to force a girl into marriage against her will,' Danielle said, but she was smiling.

'I hoped that when the time came it wouldn't really be against your will,' he said softly. 'There's something else too: if, after giving marriage a good chance, I'd realised that you were really unhappy, I would have let you go. Thing was, I had to make sure we had that chance.'

'And so you made me marry you and go away on honeymoon with you.'

'More than anything else, I hoped that by spending time alone with you I could woo you. I wanted to court you, my precious darling, to recapture the magic we'd once shared.'

'It worked, Sterling.'

'Did it, Danielle?'

'Oh, yes! I loved you more every day.'

'My darling,' Sterling said raggedly. 'Do you know, Danielle, I had planned our honeymoon even before our wedding date was set? It was to be my way of being totally alone with you, of being able to make love to you. Of trying to get you to love me as much as I loved you. For a time I even thought it was working, that you were beginning to warm to me, that things were turning out as I'd hoped.'

'Even after you knew about Toby?'

'He was a shock, I admit. For a while the thought that there'd been another man in your life nearly drove me out of my mind. I couldn't bear to think of you in another man's bed. But I loved you so much, I knew I had to spend my life with you anyway.'

'And then you saw the birthmark.'

'An even bigger shock. I was delighted, *overjoyed* that Toby was my son—there seemed to be a special bond between us almost from the moment I first met him— but I couldn't understand why you hadn't told me.'

'I'm so sorry I didn't.'

'From now on no more secrets, my darling Danielle; no more lack of trust.'

'None, I promise.'

Leaning towards her, Sterling gathered her tenderly in his arms. 'I love you so much. You're my heart, my life; I'll never let you go.'

'I love you too, my darling; I don't want to go.'

'Have you any idea how badly I want to make love to you, Danielle?'

'Why don't you?'

'Your condition.' For the first time since Danielle had known him Sterling looked uncertain.

She nuzzled her lips against his throat. 'I'm pregnant, darling, not an invalid.'

'Does that mean...?'

'We can do anything we want.'

'Toby...?'

'My parents will be delighted if we let them keep him till tomorrow.'

'Are you telling me I can spend the whole night making love to you?'

'I'm asking you to.'

'My darling Danielle! When shall we start?'

'How about now?' she asked mischievously.

They lay back on the pillows and began to kiss—special kisses, kisses like none there'd been before, because for the first time they knew that there were no limits to their lovemaking. Theirs was a love that would last for ever.

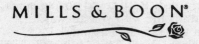

MILLS & BOON®

Next Month's Romances

♡

Each month you can choose from a wide variety of romance with Mills & Boon. Below are the new titles to look out for next month in our two new series Presents and Enchanted.

Presents™

ONE-MAN WOMAN	Carole Mortimer
MEANT TO MARRY	Robyn Donald
AUNT LUCY'S LOVER	Miranda Lee
HIS SLEEPING PARTNER	Elizabeth Oldfield
DOMINIC'S CHILD	Catherine Spencer
JILTED BRIDE	Elizabeth Power
LIVING WITH THE ENEMY	Laura Martin
THE TROPHY WIFE	Rosalie Ash

Enchanted™

NO MORE SECRETS	Catherine George
DADDY'S LITTLE HELPER	Debbie Macomber
ONCE BURNED	Margaret Way
REBEL IN DISGUISE	Lucy Gordon
FIRST-TIME FATHER	Emma Richmond
HONEYMOON ASSIGNMENT	Sally Carr
WHERE THERE'S A WILL	Day Leclaire
DESERT WEDDING	Alexandra Scott

Available from WH Smith, John Menzies, Volume One, Forbuoys, Martins, Woolworths, Tesco, Asda, Safeway and other paperback stockists.

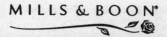

MILLS & BOON®

We value your comments!

Please spare a few moments to fill in the following questionnaire.
NO STAMP NEEDED.

Last month we introduced two new cover designs for our romance novels—Presents and Enchanted—and we'd like to know what you think. Please tick the appropriate box ☑ to indicate your answers.

---

1. How long have you been a Mills & Boon Romance reader?

Less than 1 year ☐   1-2 years ☐   3-5 years ☐
6-10 years ☐   Over 10 years ☐

2. How many Mills & Boon Romances do you read/buy in a month?

	Read	Buy
1-4	☐	☐
5-8	☐	☐
9-12	☐	☐
13-16	☐	☐
Over 17	☐	☐

3. From where do you usually obtain your Mills & Boon Romances?

Mills & Boon Reader Service ☐
WH Smith/John Menzies/Other Newsagent ☐
Supermarket ☐
Borrowed from a friend ☐
Bought from a second-hand shop ☐
Other (please specify) _____

4. Thinking about the **Presents** *cover do you:*

Like it very much ☐   Don't like it very much ☐
Like it quite a lot ☐   Don't like it at all ☐

Please turn over ☞

5. Thinking about the **Enchanted** cover do you:

Like it very much ☐   Don't like it very much ☐

Like it quite a lot ☐   Don't like it at all ☐

6. Do you have any additional comments you'd like to make about the Presents and Enchanted covers?

_____

_____

7. It is intended that the two new covers will help readers to distinguish between the different types of romantic storylines, do you think this is a good idea?

Yes ☐   No ☐

8. Are you a Reader Service subscriber?

Yes ☐   No ☐

9. Please indicate your age group

16-24 ☐   25-34 ☐   45-54 ☐   55-64 ☐   65+ ☐

Thank you for your help

Please send your completed questionnaire to:

Harlequin Mills & Boon Ltd.,
Presents/Enchanted Questionnaire,
Dept. M, FREEPOST, P.O. Box 183,
Richmond, Surrey, TW9 1ST

E1

Ms/Mrs/Miss/Mr _____

Address _____

_____

———————————— Postcode ————————————

You may be mailed with offers from other reputable companies as a result of this application. If you would prefer not to receive such offers, please tick box. ☐